Bigfoot
vs.
Chupacabra

MJ Miike

Also Published as the Memoir
"Travels with Sarai"

∞

"There are more things in heaven and earth than are dreamt
of in your philosophy."
-Wm. Shakespeare

"The ultimate authority must always rest
with the individual's own reason and critical analysis."
-The Dalai Lama

"The truth is out there."
-The X-Files

The events of this book took place over the first few months of the the year 2012, somewhere in the northern Amazon.

CHAPTER 1

Although studied in the ways of meditation, I could swear that if I have to endure this heat another hour, I will expire.

Of course, I have thought this every hour since we came down from the mountains nearly a month ago. By we, I mean myself and my traveling companion, Sarai, a brilliant naturalist and new friend, who'd been nudging me for weeks to leave the sparseness above the tree-line, which is my natural habitat, for the extreme biodiversity of the rainforest below.

Progress has been slow with Sarai by my side, who stops to take notes on nearly every plant and insect we come across. Sarai, having recently received her doctorate, is working on a grant from the National Geographic Society to catalogue new species. If she could catalogue me she would no doubt become an instant star in her field, for I should mention I am not strictly human, but a Yeti, seven feet tall and covered with snow-white fur.

How did we meet, you may be asking yourself, a legendary being from the rooftop of the world, and a post-doctoral researcher from Boston? What circumstances could possibly lead two such different creatures to become companions?

The answer is not nearly as strange as you may think. Sarai, imbued with a fearless nature and unquenchable thirst for knowledge, had contracted the services of some less-than-reputable guides in an effort to reach a remote location high in the Andes.

The guides, however, had other ideas. Kidnapping and ransom, to be precise, which is evidently far more profitable than guiding, although also far more risky, as they were soon to learn. They probably figured they had all the angles covered. What they didn't bargain on was seven feet of snow-white fur.

Suffice it to say I have certain powers that rendered the kidnappers' weapons most ineffectual. Being from Bhutan and a Yeti to boot, I am committed to non-violence, but that doesn't mean I can't give folks a well-deserved scaring. In the kidnappers' case it was especially well deserved, and while they escaped from the scene of their crime intact in body, I don't think many of them will be reviving their criminal habits, at least not for a while.

The place to which they brought her was extremely remote. Luckily for Sarai, it was also the mouth of the cave where, ensconced within, I'd been meditating for more than a month. It wasn't long before the bandits awoke me from my trance with their raucous behavior—drinking and smoking, and even, when the mood took them, shooting into the air.

I'm pretty good at meditating, having had nearly 42 years of practice, but gunfire does have a way of grabbing one's attention, especially when magnified by the natural echo chamber of a limestone cave.

It is generally not considered a good idea to go running in the direction of gunfire. The safest course of action would have been to retreat deeper into the cave until the situation on the outside resolved itself. Had I been powerless this would have been the only choice.

However, having the power to stop something potentially terrible and not exercising that power is a different thing entirely. Imagine how I would have felt, coming out of the cave when the danger had passed, to find dead bodies, knowing I could have done something. Although I had no way of knowing what was happening outside the cave, I had to investigate.

Also, I didn't go running toward the gunfire so much as creep, which I thought was a good compromise.

CHAPTER 2

I came out of the cave and the kidnappers went running. Why? The answer is simple. Simple, that is, if one is a Yeti. For it wasn't me they saw emerging from the cave, but their own deepest fears.

It's a mind trick all Yetis learn early on, as our survival depends in part on remaining mythical. I don't know what those bandits saw, for the deepest fear of each individual is, well, individual. But while I wasn't privy to what was going on in their minds, whatever it was that they saw could not have been good if the sound of their screaming, echoing up the barren slopes long after they had disappeared from view, was any indication.

This particular mind trick is sort of an area-of-effect thing—you can't pick and choose individual targets, just sort of blast everyone in the area—thus there was no way to avoid the innocent Sarai getting caught up in it.

Far from running and screaming however, such things not being in her nature even at the worst of times, Sarai had taken out her notebook and started to scribble!

You might think this is a strange reaction, I know that I did, but it makes complete sense when you find out what Sarai's deepest fear is—namely, failing to catalogue a species before it goes extinct. She even told me once that she sometimes has nightmares about it. She is obsessed with her work.

This is not to say Sarai only cares about *cataloging* species and doesn't mind if they go extinct. In fact she minds very much. The core aim of her work is meant to save such species. But saving such species in an era of industrial transformation can be very difficult, especially if that species remains unknown.

Sarai told me that scientists believe dozens of species become extinct each day due to deforestation, the majority of them never having been discovered. So instead of seeing some horror emerging from the cave, Sarai saw me as I truly am and immediately began to sketch.

At this point I found myself in a definite conundrum. Where the survival of most species in this era depends on their being known and protected, quite the opposite is true for Yetis—were there ever definitive proof of our existence, we would be overrun.

Had Sarai's purpose in cataloguing me been nefarious—a fancy way of saying evilly intentioned—I would have been justified in messing with her mind, confusing her memory of the situation so that after she couldn't be sure if it had truly happened.

This is a second technique which Yetis learn very young, for the very good reason mentioned above. As time passed she would have put it down to an hallucination caused by the high altitude, or perhaps a dream.

When a mountain climber disappears and then re-appears a few days later, disoriented and unsure of where they've been, the phenomenon is usually ascribed to the thin mountain air which plays tricks on the mind. You can bet the real truth is they've run into a Yeti.

This confusion technique is justified because the first thought most people have on seeing a Yeti is "this is going to make me rich!" Though it's not an evil thought in the strictest sense, in the context it is so potentially harmful, it qualifies them for the memory scramble.

Sarai's intent, however, was highly altruistic—a fancy way of saying selflessly good—and thus it would have been highly questionable, morally speaking, to mess with her mind in such a manner. My only option was to sit down and talk, hoping she would understand.

This turned out to be the best thing I'd done since leaving the remote mountains of my birth.

CHAPTER 3

I was on the Yeti version of *'Rumspringa'*, a period
between childhood and adulthood when young Yetis roam
the earth. The purpose of this journey is to expand one's
horizons, to grow and learn, outside of the confines of
school. While school has many benefits, it's sphere is largely
limited to what can be found in books. I can certainly
vouch for the value of books, particularly for the hungry
mind, nevertheless there is no substitute for the knowledge
gained from experience. Thus the purpose of the journey
to gain such experience and bring it back for the benefit of
the entire community.

Up to this point, my travels had been relatively uneventful: first coming down from the high Himalayas by hidden paths unknown to men, streams becoming rivers, cutting through untrammeled gorges on their unending journeys down to the sea; next floating on a hand-made raft of sturdy bamboo to the Antarctic Continent, which I crossed on foot with nothing but a shoulder-load of seaweed for sustenance; finally drifting by means of an ice raft to the southern-most tip of South America, where upon arrival I made straight for the high mountains and began trekking north.

I had expected to find many new things on my journey, but nothing so intriguing as a Sarai! She promptly dubbed me Homo Hirsutus, which is Latin for "hairy human", and later when we came across various branches in the evolutionary tree and further classification was needed, Homo Hirsutus Nivosa, which means "snowy-haired human".

It didn't take me long to convince her that to reveal my species would be disastrous for us. In fact it didn't take much convincing—Sarai understood the problem and agreed to keep it to herself. For it is quite a different thing to discover a new plant or bird, and a highly intelligent, humanoid species, by all accounts held to be mythical.

In exchange for her silence (well, maybe not strictly in exchange because Sarai wasn't expecting anything in return—she simply saw it was the right thing to do) I agreed to accompany her in her travels; part guide, part bodyguard.

Sarai immediately saw the advantages of this—a creature like me could lead her to places otherwise inaccessible to most Humans.[1] For me it was a chance to learn first-hand about Humans, knowledge that could well prove useful upon my eventual return to my people.

There was another factor however, one for which I was completely unprepared—being around Sarai also made me feel good! More on this later.

---

[1] For the purposes of clarity, when I use "Humans" with a capital H, I am referring to Homo Sapiens; when "humans" with a lowercase h, the greater "Homo" genus which includes Yetis and other such species.

CHAPTER 4

Now, seven feet tall may sound impressive to you, but I assure you that for Yetis it is considered on the short side, so I've always been a little self-conscious about my appearance. Yeti[2] are supposed to be above these kinds of concerns, but there you have it.

The irony now was, compared now to Sarai, I felt like a lunk—huge, hulking and rather ungainly. Awkward would be a good way to put it.

Worse yet, because I'm covered with fur, I have no sweat glands. This means when I'm out of my natural

---

[2] The proper plural noun for "Yeti" is "Yeti", although I have taken the liberty of using the colloquial "Yetis" in most cases as it sounds more natural to the ear. It is my hope this will not cause confusion. (But if it does, just put it down to your run-in with a Yeti ;)

habitat, specifically the cold of the highest altitudes, I have to pant in order to keep cool.

Despite my years of meditation training in which you learn to suppress the ego, with Sarai I found the need to pant incredibly embarrassing. Worse yet, Sarai can't help but giggle every time she's looked at me since we came down from the mountains!

I know she doesn't mean to make me feel bad because she always kisses me to let me know she's only teasing, not in a romantic way, mind, more the way you'd kiss a dog. I have to admit I find it quite pleasant, and also for some reason, slightly disappointing.

For although I am 42 years old, for my species, who live an average of 400 years, this is barely into adolescence, equivalent to a Human, say, of twelve or thirteen.

CHAPTER 5

We'd been wandering in circles for days. By this I
don't mean to say looping our actual progress, as in
returning to the same spot, but that the path we were on
was really large and circular.

If you've ever trekked through a dense forest, and
there is no forest denser than a tropical rainforest, you'll
know that it's hard to keep your bearings in the best
conditions. The path we were on was clearly designed to
exacerbate this problem—it's curvature was of a degree that
makes it easy to mistake the direction, and the subtle
branchings off the path were designed to appear counter-
intuitive. This meant you'd choose the fork that seemed

correct, only to end up losing ground. All of which was interesting indeed.

For there was something familiar in this labyrinthine design, something reminiscent of the paths my people make to confuse mountaineers and keep them from our homes.

In fact, that really famous labyrinth you've no doubt heard of—the infamous trap designed by Daedalus for the Cretan King Minos—was passed down to *them* from my people on Atlantis, back before it returned to the stars.[3]

The original labyrinth was merely a spiral, designed to make the journey to it's center as arduous as possible. Thus, when the unlucky person forced to walk it reached the center, they were weary, famished, and ready to drop.

At the center of the Atlantean labyrinth was what is sometimes called "the Great Mystery", not a thing but an experience, the nature of which I can't go into for the obvious reasons of it being mysterious and me not knowing myself.

At the center of the Cretan labyrinth was a Bull-Human hybrid with a taste for human flesh, which is a pretty good example of the uses Humans tend to think up for things, and part of the reason we Yeti keep our distance.

---

[3] Contrary to popular belief, reports of that legendary city sinking beneath the waves are greatly exaggerated.

The labyrinth I and Sarai were on was winding unhurriedly toward the heart of the jungle, but as I mentioned, if you didn't know what you were doing, you'd end up literally walking in circles. Luckily, I did know what I was doing and so we were making steady progress.

So I can't say I was surprised when a Sasquatch, otherwise known as a Bigfoot, came tearing along the path. In fact, I was sort of expecting it. What I wasn't expecting was the cause for the Bigfoot's haste—for he blew past us at a pace that made my fur rustle, never pausing for so much as a "how do you do"—revealed a moment later to be a screeching pack of what I at first took to be rabid monkeys.

Now, I want to tell you that's something you don't see every day.

CHAPTER 6

I later found out the rabid monkeys weren't monkeys at all, but Chupacabras, the legendary "goat suckers" of the Latin world.

When most people think Chupacabra, they think of the numerous notorious cases of goats found dead, completely drained of blood.

While these blood-drained goats were almost certainly victims of Chupacabras, the descriptions that make the Chupacabras out to look like scabrous, mangy coyotes are not exactly accurate.

First of all, Chupacabras are nothing like coyotes, except, I suppose, for the fangs. Sarai's guess is they evolved from something like a baboon, which is a kind of primate with extremely menacing, canine teeth.

The hands and feet of the Chupacabras are sort of like a sloth's, which have really long finger and toenails, good for hanging on to trees. While Chupacabras also like to hang from trees, they find the skill even more efficacious for hanging onto prey, goats popularly, while slurping down a meal of nice, fresh blood, although goats are not their native food source.

The Chupacabras' eyes are gleaming red, which gives them a somewhat menacing aspect, but other than that, they look pretty much like little people covered with fur. A new species of Homo Hirsutus, Homo Hirsutus Brevis, which is latin for "Hairy Little People", so dubbed by Sarai.

Probably the worst thing about them is their smell which can be quite terrible, and that's understatement. I later found out this is partly because they like to roll themselves in dung, which allows them to approach their prey without disturbing it, and partly because they never took a bath. You could say they have a lot stacked against them socially.

As the wild, smelly pack raced by us, hot on the tail of the lone Bigfoot, Sarai and I tumbled into the undergrowth.

Then, after sharing an astonished look, we took off running after them.

In no time at all we came to a clearing where the Bigfoot, no longer running, was attempting unsuccessfully to shake off the the more than a dozen screeching Chupacabras that were clinging to its body, biting, scratching, and crapping.

When you see a sight like that, even if you're a Yeti with mystical powers, there's a part of you that's screaming, "RUN!!"

Instead, I composed myself and began to hum.

CHAPTER 7

If you're wondering why I was humming, I want to tell you it was not for entertainment purposes. For all the flaws I may have, I'm not going to just stand there, humming my favorite song while a poor, lone Bigfoot gets mauled by a pack of vicious Chupacabras. In fact, what I was humming wasn't even a tune.

What I was doing was more like a sonic blast—a type of harmonic resonance that can stun, paralyze, and even kill. If you've ever heard the legendary throat-singers of Tuva, it's kind of like that, only times about a thousand.

As I emitted the sonic burst, the swarm of Chupacabras at once went limp, hanging listlessly from the relieved and astonished Bigfoot.

Sarai, who was safely behind me and thus out of the path of the sonic blast, had recovered in record time from the shock of seeing two more previously undocumented, mythical species and was frantically scribbling in her notebook.

"Frrbrgr! Thought I was a goner for sure!" Growled the Bigfoot in a language I recognized as a distant dialect of my own.

"Are you alright?" I asked.

"A goner for sure! M' whole body feels 'a sleepin', Frrbrg."

I attempted to assure him the effects of the blast would soon wear off.

The frequency I had used was just right for stunning the little Chupacabras, but on a creature as big as the Bigfoot who was at least nine feet tall, it had an effect similar to when your leg "falls asleep", only for your entire body.

I know this because Yeti children have a game similar to your Human "tag" where instead of touching someone to make them "it," you freeze them with a sonic burst.

We began picking Chupacabras off of the Bigfoot, laying them on the jungle floor where Sarai could examine them.

"Damned interesting." Muttered Sarai, inspecting the snoozing Chupacabras.

"Frrbrgr." said the Bigfoot in a surly tone.

I was starting to realize this Bigfoot was not so much in the brains department, if you take my meaning, but nothing prepared me for what he did next, which was to start stomping Chupacabras with his gargantuan foot.

Bigfoots, as the name implies, have really, really, really big feet (and yes, "Bigfoots" is the proper plural). Being the largest known hominids, Bigfoots are extremely strong, but it's their feet that you have to really watch out for. If a Bigfoot gets you under foot, it's all over.[4]

I must have been in shock at the suddenness of the Bigfoot's assault, violence being anathema to Yetis, and so I just stood there dumbly, mouth hanging open, as he squashed the defenseless Chupacabras like melons.

---

[4] For the Bigfoots Sarai finally settled on *Homo Hirsutus Magnapedis*, which is Latin for "Hairy Humans with Great Big Feet".

CHAPTER 8

Sarai, perhaps more accustomed to the brutality of nature, was the first to react. By the time I'd recovered from my initial shock, she was pummeling the Bigfoot's back with her fists, screaming "Stop! You're killing them!"

Thankfully, the Bigfoot was so big and bulky that he barely noticed her pummeling fists. For if he had and had taken it badly, he could have broken her back with a swat of his hand—while Bigfoot hands are nothing compared to their feet, they are nonetheless quite impressive.

I pulled Sarai off, planted my foot, and knocked the Bigfoot with my shoulder.

Just because we Yeti practice non-violence doesn't mean we don't learn how to fight—sometimes staying healthy requires knocking an attacker on their butt.

"There's no reason to harm them now!" I shouted.

"Plenny reason." The Bigfoot said. "Plenny Frrbrgrr!"

He went to stomp another defenseless Chupacabra, but I pressed against him so he was just off balance enough so as not to be able to bring down his foot.

The Bigfoot wasn't quite sure what was going on, but it was clear he wasn't going to give up, so I finally knocked him on his big, hairy Bigfoot butt.

This didn't stop him and he kept trying to get up and get at the Chupacabras, so I kept pushing him backwards to keep him off-balance. This was quite surprising to the Bigfoot, who was a good two feet taller than me and clearly much stronger.

Though we share a common ancestor, we Yetis gave up brawn for brains in the great march of evolutionary progress, while Bigfoots remained much like our ancient ancestors: big, strong, and not so much in the mental department.

However, we Yeti, having our brains to compensate for our relative lack of brawn, have developed a martial arts system very similar to your Human Tai Chi. In fact, Tai Chi's principles are based on our art, taught in ancient times to a certain buddhist mystic who was making his way from India to China. This martial method focuses on yielding and redirection rather than brute force, and properly utilized, it is extremely effective. The downside is it takes 30 years to learn, but luckily I began training at 12.

When the remaining Chupacabras started to stir, I began once again to hum. This was not to knock them back out—I certainly did not want to see any more defenseless creatures harmed by the Bigfoot, vicious or no—but merely to discourage further attack. Luckily, they'd had enough and melted into the jungle, taking with them their dead.

This was one of the first indications we were dealing with a truly human species, care for the dead being a strictly human trait. It's also a reason there is no direct evidence of humanoid cryptids—no bodies are left behind.

While the threat of renewed Chupacabra attack was now diffused, the same could not be said for the smell which unfortunately lingered, covered as the Bigfoot was— and now Sarai and I were per our efforts to stop the Bigfoot's stomping—with saliva, mucous, and yes, even Chupa poop.

CHAPTER 9

It's a good thing I'm covered with fur, because
otherwise I'm pretty sure I would have turned bright red.
The reason for this was that as we came to a stream where
we could wash off the various Chupa effluvia, Sarai
unceremoniously stripped off her clothing and waded into
the stream.

I had never seen a naked woman before and for some
reason I couldn't quite seem to tear my eyes away. This
wouldn't seem to make much sense since we were
completely different species—which must have been her
assumption also as she appeared completely unconcerned,
bathing there in the altogether—but there was something
mesmerizing about her natural form.

"Well, what are you waiting for, stinky!" Sarai called.

"Heh." I replied sheepishly, looking away and wading into the stream.

The Bigfoot on the other hand—whose name we later learned was in fact Frrbrgr—was as unconcerned with Sarai's natural state as he seemingly was with the terrible smell emanating from his fur, and he just squatted by the bank muttering to himself as we washed ourselves clean.

Once we were cleansed and properly de-stinkified, sunning ourselves on the stream's mossy bank, we learned from Frrbrgr that the Chupacabras had been invading the Bigfoot territory, attacking without warning and causing all sorts of trouble. Two Bigfoots had even been badly mauled, a fate Frrbrgr had escaped only per our timely intercession.

This was revealed in a roundabout way, there being the triple challenges of Bigfoots not being overly eloquent, me being soggy since I had been too self-conscious with Sarai there to shake the water out of my fur, and Sarai being still in her natural state as she waited for her clothes to dry.

The first factor meant I had to piece together the story based on grunts and one-word answers which can be quite maddening; the second factor made it harder to hear because my ear fur was so sodden; but it was the third factor, that of Sarai's natural state, which I found most distracting, and it made it hard to think clearly, this despite the Yeti's legendary powers of concentration.

"Ratmen bad!" Frrbrgr was very emphatic on this point, 'Ratmen' being the Bigfoot name for the Chupacabras. "Very, very bad."

CHAPTER 10

We arrived at the Bigfoot village in the late afternoon. It was a ramshackle affair in a less dense part of the forest.

The houses were rude lean-tos, which are a primitive kind of shelter made from branches and leaves. No fire pits were evident, that element evidently not being necessary.

In fact, if no one told you it was a village, you'd probably just think it was a bunch of broken tree branches strewn about a clearing.

They didn't need much shelter, being made like all fur-covered things to live in harmony with the elements, and this region in particular being quite temperate.

There were about a dozen Bigfoots living in the village, not including the Bigfoot children, who were difficult to count. The boys being prone to constant, frenzied activity, usually in a pile up all together, and the girls given to randomly disappearing, there was no way to really tell how many they were.

It was the wounded adults though, who really got may attention, oozing from multiple open wounds, both bites and deep scratches. Small as they may be, these Chupacabras are no joke!

Apparently there had been a bit of a scuffle with the Chupacabras a few nights prior with Bigfoots coming off the worse, and the mood in the village was decidedly grim.

Frrbrgr took us to the Bigfoot I took to be in charge, a towering ten-footer called Grrbrgr, who eyed me with suspicion.

Frrbrgr whispered into Grrbrgr's ear and Grrbrgr didn't look happy with what Frrbrgr was telling him.

"You no hum, fight Grrbrgr fair." Grrbrgr said

I started to explain that I was not here to fight but to help the Bigfoots with their Chupacabra problem.

"Help after. Fight first. GRR!!!!"

With that Grrbrgr charged, barely giving me time to sidestep and get my bearings.

I learned later that in Bigfoot society, whenever a new male comes of age or appears, he has to fight the dominant male, sort of like dogs fighting to establish the pack hierarchy. In other words, determine who's in charge. As soon as the Alpha is established, whether the old boss or the new, peace and order are instantly restored.

I knew this wasn't going to make my kind look particularly good to Sarai and I made a mental note to tell her later that no such custom existed in Yeti society—at least not for hundreds of thousands of years!

Sarai later commented that the Bigfoots didn't seem like the "brightest bulbs in the socket." I didn't get the reference at first, never having see a lightbulb up close, but I eventually worked out that it was a Human variant on our Yeti "not the sharpest stalagmite in the cave."

At the present, however, I had bigger things occupying my mind—namely ten feet of Bigfoot to fight, and let me tell you that means ten feet of pure muscle and fur. It's true Grrbrgr was stronger than me—a lot stronger, actually, being a good three feet taller and couple hundred pounds heavier—and that he fought with a terrifying fury.

It's natural you might think this would be an advantage—and it could have been if Grrbrgr's opponent was not a trained fighter—but on this day Grrbrgr's opponent was me.

Anger is proven to reduce IQ, and these Bigfoots were already somewhat deficient in that category. This made Grrbrgr's movements very easy to predict and allowed me to avoid him with ease. His confidence in his greater size and strength also clearly led him to underestimate me.

But as I say, he was strong—very, very strong—and while he could not lay his hands on me, neither could I overcome him.

The clear solution was to wear him down, the only problem being that the longer I fought in this steamy rainforest, the hotter I would get, and the hotter I got, the more I would pant. Thus, in addition to being forced to act like a dog, I would also look like one, with Sarai observing the whole embarrassing spectacle.

Luckily, while incredibly strong, Bigfoots are not made for sustained activity. (In fact, we came to learn they are extremely lazy. More on this later.) Let it just be said for now that this trait was a blessing that day, as soon both I and Grrbrgr were so darn tired, we didn't have any energy to fight, and just stood there panting.

A huge grin crossed Grrbrgr's face and offered me his big, paw-like hand. Incredibly relieved, I smiled and took his hand in my own.

Perhaps, despite the earlier spectacle, Sarai would believe that we hairy humans could be civilized after all.

The next thing I knew, I was flat on my back, seeing stars.

CHAPTER 11

Sarai told me later I had been "sucker-punched", a technique of dirty fighting my Yeti training had in no way prepared me for.[5] I promised myself I would not be so easy to dupe in future!

However, in the context of the situation, it seemed to be just the thing. Grrbrgr was now being extremely friendly, the tribe hierarchy having been duly re-established, and he introduced me to the other Bigfoots like we were the oldest of pals.

---

[5] This illustrates my point on the difference between scholastic learning and real-world experience. While my dojo training had given me an effective martial art, the formalized approach approach was not a guarantee of success on the streets, or in this case, the jungle, as the present circumstances clearly revealed.

That the victory had been won by a dirty trick did not seem to factor in, which was fine with me because it meant that at least now I could try to figure out what was going on between the Chupacabras and the Bigfoots.

I began to be aware of being intensely watched and soon noticed three female Bigfoots smiling at me in a most suggestive manner.

"Now Wife choose!" Grrbrgr commanded with a huge grin, slapping me on the back like the best of buddies. "This Mùlululu, Lùlululu, and Mulùlululu. Nice, yes? Lucky Cloud Hair!"

"What's he saying?" Sarai whispered at me.

"I think he's offering, uhhh—" I had to look away in embarrassment. "He appears to be asking me to choose a wife?"

"Go get 'em, Tiger." Sarai whispered with a huge grin on her face.

To say that I was shocked at her response would be an understatement of understatements, and it must have been written all over my own face.

"Just kidding." Sarai whispered back. "But are you going to?"

"Of course not!" I retorted indignantly.

Once again, I was glad I was covered with silky fur.

"I am most appreciative. Your offer is extremely generous." I said to Grrbrgr, "But no such thanks is necessary."

"No thanks? You kidding? Insult Lovely!?" Grrbrgr was starting to get angry again.

"No, no. They are very lovely." I assured him. "But under the circumstances, well, you see..."

I'd be lying if I said some part of me wasn't tempted. Primitive though these evolutionary cousins of mine may have been, the Bigfoot females, who are even bigger than the males and twice as hairy, were in fact rather fetching, which is an old-fashioned and fancy way of saying quite pretty.

One of the Bigfoot females (either Mùlululu or Lùlululu, although it could have been Mulùlululu—I hadn't quite gotten straight who was who) batted her enormous eyelashes at me.

I feel I have to take a moment to describe the extraordinary eye-lashes of the Bigfoot female.

It is their most obvious gender trait, aside from the extra size and hairiness, and what a trait!

The lashes of the Bigfoot female are just, well, enchanting, and I mean this in the most literal sense of the word.

Long as caterpillars and iridescent, their graceful "just so" arcs catch the light sparkling down through the forest canopy and shimmer in a mesmerizing way—each lash its own little rainbow—and when they flutter it is like a swarm of butterflies rising up to greet the dawn. Marvelous. Dazzling. Resplendent.[6]

My mouth had fallen open in awe, and who knows what might have happened had Sarai not been present—me never having had to deal with a situation even remotely close to this—but I knew I would never do anything that would diminish me in Sarai's eyes.

I shook my head and my wits returned, sort of.

With some effort I was able to turn back to Grrbrgr and I eventually got him to relent, although only because he came to believe that Sarai was my wife! (This I know because he recounted it to the tribe, drawing many astonished gasps.)

After that all the Bigfoots looked at me with great sympathy, clearly regarding me as incredibly unfortunate to

---

[6] I have since seen several "Hoochie Women" during our sojourn in L.A., but even the most extreme and ornate of false eyelashes are nothing compared to the wondrous eyelashes of the Bigfoot female.

Another interesting feature is that they are born with their eyelashes at full size and luster, thus that the littler the Bigfoot girl, the bigger the eyelashes in relation to the rest of her. Cute does not begin to describe it. All I can say is I hope you are lucky enough to one day witness them for yourself!

have been saddled with so scrawny and hairless a wife, which I know for certain because it was the subject of many hushed conversations over the course of the night.

When Sarai asked me what they were saying I told her they thought she was scrawny.

"Haha. They think I'm skinny. Excellent." Said Sarai.

I had initially taken Grrbrgr's proposition as offering me one of three Bigfoot females, but it turns out that Bigfoots, having a male to female ratio of roughly 6:1, practice a custom known as 'polyandry'. This is to say that each wife had several husbands.

"I'm starting to like these Bigfoots more by the minute." Quipped Sarai when I explained it to her.

Despite the having of six husbands per, these Bigfoot Wives did not seem at all unenthusiastic about the prospect of taking on another. The way Mulùlululu (or was it Mùlululu or Lùlululu?) was eyeing me was actually making me feel a little uncomfortable.

At one point during our stay she even tried to trade Sarai one of her Bigfoot husbands for me!

At first I refused to translate, but Sarai kept bugging me until I told her.

"Yep. More and more by the minute." said Sarai.

And for the third time that day, I was glad I was covered with a thick coat of fur.

CHAPTER 12

Having thus been accepted by the tribe, I was immediately popular. Novelties of any kind must have been rare in that neck of the woods, and snow-white Yetis virtually unheard of. So I was poked, prodded, sniffed, and even licked, by the entire Bigfoot tribe. I seemed especially popular with the Bigfoot children, who were climbing all over me nearly the entire night.

Conversely, Sarai, they didn't seem to regard much at all, except to eye her suspiciously. Soon enough though they forgot all about her and began to treat her much the way I suspect a human treats a pet. By this I mean they would pat her absently when they passed by. I have to admit, the irony of this reversal of roles made me smile inwardly just the littlest bit.

The situation suited Sarai just fine, as it left her free to watch the Bigfoots go about their business, and she spent the whole time happily scribbling in her notebook, which you now are realizing is pretty much all she does when she's not sleeping or hiking.

That night the Bigfoots laid out a huge feast. When I say "laid out" I mean this literally. They knocked down a fairly sizable tree that had started to go rotten and dragged it into the center of the village. The repast consisted of the rich variety of insects living in the tree and surprisingly, the tree itself, which is to say the leaves and bark and the soft, rotted wood.

This is part of the reason Bigfoots are so lazy—when you can wake up the morning and grab a nice leafy stick for breakfast, you can afford to be.

"You help kill Ratmen." Grrbrgr said, sucking the goo from the carapace of a still-struggling spider the size of his fist. "Ratmen bad, Grrbrgr, mmph, slurp."

It was difficult for me to watch Grrbrgr eat a living insect. Intellectually I knew that the spider's brain was nothing more than a cluster of neurons, a set of instinctual behaviors largely devoted to the spinning of webs, that the spider was not capable of any higher functions such as the ability to feel horror at it's ghastly fate, and yet I could not help but help feel a pang as I witnessed its suffering. I had to turn away and look at a tree while I answered Grrbrgr.

"Perhaps there is a solution other than violence." I suggested. "The forest is very big. Surely there must be room for both Bigfoot and Ratmen."

Grrbrgr fell back laughing uproariously, as did all the Bigfoots, rolling on their backs, gasping for breath, tears of laughter streaming from their eyes.

"White-Hair not smart! White-Hair talk to tree!" Grrbrgr roared with delight, all the Bigfoots hooting and hollering along with him.

Eventually they settled down and I was able to turn the conversation back toward the subject at hand, namely finding a peaceful resolution to the conflict with the Chupacabras.

"NO!" Roared Grrbrgr. "Bigfoots mind own business. Ratmen attack. Ratmen bad! Grr-Br-Gr!"

This last bit, apparently, for emphasis, as Grrbrgr was so worked up, he crushed the poor spider in his mammoth fist and stomped off into the forest where we heard him crashing and smashing for a long while after.

Sarai gave me a sympathetic look and said, "Guess somebody's having a bad day."

I could see it was going to be difficult to get Grrbrgr to see the possibility of a negotiated solution, and I can't say I didn't see his point. The Chupacabras did come across as somewhat vicious. Still they were human beings, primitive as they may be, and thus might be reasoned with.

Without Grrbrgr to negotiate with there was nothing to be done but wait, so I settled in and watched the Bigfoots.

One immediate difference I noticed between Bigfoots and Yetis is a practice which Sarai later told me was called 'social grooming.'

Yetis, living as we do in the remotest mountains far above the treeline, have no issues with parasitic insects, one of the great advantages of living at such high altitudes.

Bigfoots, on the other hand, are walking insect infestations. 'Flea ridden' only begins to describe it. I eventually realized the grooming is not so much because they mind the fleas, but that they regard them as a tasty snack, and the grooming of one's pals as an entertaining pastime.

If it sounds crazy to you that picking fleas out of your buddy's hair and crunching them between your teeth is an entertaining pastime, just remember that they have no TV. I should also mention the fleas were as big as crickets, so a Bigfoot could get a decent snack out of delousing a pal.

You're probably thinking this is a pretty sorry existence, but you have to weigh the pros and cons.

Sure, Bigfoots don't have all the modern conveniences of Humans, but then they lead pretty stress-free lives. The reason Humans need so many conveniences is because they spend all of their time working! In other words, they spend all their time working in order to earn the money to pay for all conveniences that they wouldn't need in the first place if they didn't have to work all the time!

Before you judge others, make sure to turn the mirror on yourself.

The Bigfoot children, less interested in the sedentary pastime of grooming, had a game that seemed to involve kicking around a dead raccoon, then smashing it to a pulp with sticks.[7]

As the evening progressed, I noticed several Bigfoots huddled around a tree at the edge of the settlement. When I ambled over to investigate, I saw they were engaged in a gambling activity known as "throwing bones." While for Humans, "bones" would be merely a euphemism for dice, that is, a colorful way of describing the activity, for Bigfoots

---

[7] Sarai later told me it was a *Coatimundi*, a type of raccoon native to the South American rainforest, luckily, not endangered. At least not yet.

there was nothing euphemistic about it—what they were throwing were actual bones, knuckle bones from the looks of them.

Primitive though the Bigfoots may have been, I was nevertheless unable to follow the rules, which seemed to comprise of a dizzying array of bets and side bets, all proceeding at a breakneck pace. Any attempt to garner an explanation was met with grunts, no Bigfoot willing to tear their attention away from the gambling.

I was not surprised that the "money" being used were the large, cricket-sized Bigfoot fleas. To this end each Bigfoot had hollowed out a gourd, stopping up the tops with their massive thumbs in order to keep the fleae from escaping, then shaking them out when they needed more of the feisty insects to bet with.[8]

Although I didn't take part in the gambling myself, it was quite interesting to watch. A Bigfoot would shake the bones in his massive fist, sometimes blowing on the bones for luck, then throw them down on a huge shiny leaf, at which point some would groan, others would cheer, and

---

[8] The only downside to this storage system was there was no way to tell how many fleas were in any given gourd aside from shaking it and estimating. As you may have guessed, math is not on of the Bigfoot's strong suits, so it was not uncommon for a Bigfoot to come up empty and fly into a rage, flinging the gourd in exasperation, before desperately digging into their own fur in hopes of finding a few overlooked parasites.

there would be much haggling and scrabbling over the fleas as they changed from one gourd to the other.

Grrbrgr didn't return to the village until very late that night and I thought it best to suspend our conversation until the morning when we'd all had a chance to sleep on things. I was hoping that by the light of day I'd be able to get him to see reason.

We bedded down for the evening on the edge of the village, Sarai snuggling into my fur as she hadn't done since we left the freezing nights of the mountains. I thought this a prudent decision, surrounded as we were by hairy, feral people several times her size, but I'd be lying if I said it didn't make me feel elated, in a somewhat perplexing way, deep down inside.

CHAPTER 13

The next morning all the Bigfoots were happily finishing off the last of the rotted tree. A full belly makes a fine friend, and with everyone in such good spirits, I thought it would be the perfect opportunity to propose to Grrbrgr my intent seek out the Chupacabras and try to solve the problem.

Grrbrgr was very happy at this, which surprised me at first, until it became clear that by 'solve' he believed I meant wipe them out.

Many of the Bigfoots wanted to come along, assuming, like Grrbrgr, that I was going to wage war (and probably thinking there'd be plenty of helpless Chupacabras to stomp), but I let on that what I was planning to do would be easier if I went alone, which was absolutely true, despite their misconceptions.

In fact, the idea of reconciliation seemed quite beyond the Bigfoot capacity for reason. In their estimation, the solution to every problem was to smash and stomp, especially stomp, despite the fact that it didn't seem to be working out so well for them at the moment.

Before you become judgmental on the subject, I feel I should point out that Humans are not much more advanced in the area of peacemaking, preferring in all too many instances to 'shoot first and ask questions later'.

In any event, I didn't see any point in disabusing Grrbrgr or the other Bigfoots of their misconception at this stage, so I merely asked them to point me in the right direction.

It was still bright and early when Sarai and I set off for the heart of Chupacabra territory. At first, progress was easy and I figured we'd be there in no time, but very soon covering ground was exponentially more difficult.

Where Bigfoot paths are quite roomy for someone my size, the Chupacabra paths were little more that tunnels in the undergrowth, that is, when they were on the ground at all. As I mentioned before, the Cabras have claws designed for hanging onto things, and thus they were just as happy making their way through the treetops as the jungle floor.

There is a little song I can sing that surrounds my body with a gentle sort of force-field, something my people use when caught in particularly fearsome blizzard to keep from getting trapped and buried. It works like a charm on snow before it has a chance to become packed, and in the jungle I'd found it also works wonders in the delousing department. A verse or two and all the little mites rise unharmed from one's hide and go seek their fortunes elsewhere.

This song worked up to a point in the thick jungle brush, parting the foliage in front of us, but for the most part the growth was so thick and tangled, even the song could not force it apart.

The other problem with the song was that, although it parted the foliage in front of us, allowing passage—albeit increasingly difficult passage—there was also the effect of the foliage *closing in* behind us as we progressed.

Thus we were eventually stuck, pressed against each other in a mat of intertwined vines both before and behind.

"Another fine mess you've got us into." Sarai remarked.[9]

You might be thinking 'they could just tear out the vines', believing perhaps that vines are weak. And while it is true I could have torn any individual vine, trying to tear them when they're tangled together is another thing entirely. To make matters worse, the vines weren't just before and behind us, they were also above and below. It was sort of like being dragged down by a river of rope.

It was easy to see how the Chupacabras had been able to remain so isolated, even from other such mythical creatures as Bigfoots, living as the Cabras did in the densest part of the forest.

I had never been in such a situation, being as I am from the rooftop of the world and more used to dealing with black ice and avalanches, and I was completely at a loss as to how to remedy it. This is not meant as an excuse, just that it was out of my previous range of experience.

While I was pondering this, Sarai, business as usual, was wriggling and shimmying—a not at all unpleasant sensation, pressed as closely as she was against my back with all of the requisite feminine attributes. Unfortunately,

---

[9] A quote I later learned this was from a series of early Hollywood movies about another set of unlikely companions called 'Laurel and Hardy'. I subsequently saw several of these films during our time in Los Angeles and I thought they were quite entertaining.

it seemed to have the effect of shutting *off* my brain, which was precisely the opposite of what I needed!

Then, before I knew what was happening, Sarai had freed her machete and started hacking away at the vines.

It took nearly an hour for her to create enough of a clearing to allow us a practical degree of mobility, and soon she was hacking a path through the dense jungle brush. The problem was, after another hour of hard exertion, we'd barely covered five feet of ground.

Sarai was dripping with sweat, and by dripping, I mean dripping.

"Whew-wee!" Exclaimed Sarai, sniffing herself, "I smell worse than a Chupacabra!"

Privately I disagreed, finding her particular scent more than agreeable. However, I thought it prudent not to comment on this, and instead said, "I guess sometimes panting has its advantages."

Sarai fixed me with a penetrating look. Then her face became tender.

"I'm sorry for giggling at you so much." She said earnestly. "It's just you're so darn cute with that great big tongue of yours lolling around like that!"

Before I could form a response, she dug her hands deep into my furry sideburns and gave me big kiss right in the center of my forehead.

CHAPTER 14

Now I've spoken about my complicated feelings regarding Sarai's friendly kisses, which though always welcome, were also vaguely disappointing. However, in the current circumstance, the kiss had an effect that can only be described as magical.

If you know anything about Shakti yoga, a practice first developed by the Yeti in Atlantis, you will know that the center of the forehead is also the position of an energy point, or 'chakra', known as the "Third Eye". All creatures have one, though it is more developed in some species than others. (Humans can certainly develop it, although all too often they seem to prefer keeping it tightly shut.)

Although I hadn't been aware of it previously, the oppressive heat of the lowland jungle, compounded by the recent, surprising events—and if I am being completely honest, my confusing feeling towards Sarai—had the cumulative effect of slowly closing my third eye.

I don't mean to brag either about how open my third eye had been before—by Yeti standards my third eye development was intermediate at best, and that's being generous.

Nevertheless, Sarai's innocent kiss, filled with the energy of true compassion, popped that third eye of mine right back open. In fact, it popped it open a whole lot wider than it had been before! If you've never experienced this, all I can say is it's akin to flipping on one of your human lightbulbs in a pitch dark basement, only to discover the lightbulb is the blazing sun and you are at the top of a soaring mountain.

All of a sudden the jungle no longer seemed an obstacle, but instead a brilliant puzzle. Where before I'd only seen impossibly tangled undergrowth, I now saw the areas *in between*. The interstices, if you want to get fancy. The effect of this was that what had been once was an impassible barrier was now merely the framing of a very clear path.

I was eager to explain what had occurred to Sarai, who sat sprawled on a vine bed, grimly taking measure of what lay ahead. However, every time I tried to phrase it—having to do as it did with the kiss—it came out sounding all wrong. I felt in this case it was better to let it go for the moment.

For the side-effect of the opening of my third eye was to also clear the cobwebs from my mind, those 'cobwebs' specifically relating to my complicated feelings for my plucky companion Sarai.

This is to say that the root of those complicated feelings came from a subtle interaction of hormones and pheromones. In other words, the body, as opposed to the clear rationality of the liberated mind. My own inexperience with matters of the flesh had further compounded things, because while they talk about it a lot in Yeti school, in fact, it's an entire subject—having someone tell you about it and experiencing it for yourself are two very different things.

In the instant that my third eye popped back open, the futility of such emotionally loaded feelings as desire were revealed to me quite plainly. There is, of course, a certain romance attached to such feelings, but more often than not, they lead to all kinds of trouble.

Realizing this brought a sense of detachment, like a world being lifted from my weary shoulders, though not without—again if I am being completely honest—a certain degree of wistfulness for my earlier naivety. Oh, the irony!

Instead of trying to explain all this, I merely said, "I see a path."

"Really?" retorted Sarai. "Forgive me if I am skeptical."

I tapped the center of my forehead and said, "Just had to see things in the right way."

Then, to her complete astonishment, I began striding almost comfortably through the once impassible landscape.

"For a big galoot, you really are something," Sarai said, padding softly along the carpet of vines behind me.

CHAPTER 15

Our almost magical progress through the jungle brush brought us to the Chupacabra settlement sooner than expected. I use the word 'settlement' because they were definitely settled, although unlike the Bigfoot village, there were no dwellings in the Human sense. In fact, the dwelling of the Chupacabras was nothing more than a giant tree, and when I say giant, I mean really, really big. In fact it wasn't so much a single tree as several trees fused together with the massive root base twisting out to form a village-sized clearing. Above, the spreading branches and thick leaves formed a perfect canopy that hid the Chupacabras, both from the sun above and from curious eyes below.

Thus it was not any visual cue that let us know we were approaching the Chupacabra settlement, but the *smell*. Even being upwind as we were, it was an unmistakable. (Sarai later dubbed it the 'magnificent stink'.) But any advantage conferred by being upwind from the vantage of stink relief was cancelled out by the fact of *being upwind*, which meant that despite the Chupacabras being mostly asleep in the late afternoon, hanging upside down from the shady branches, they smelled us before we smelled them.

As we entered the clearing the tree was coming alive, buzzing with the sound of hundreds of Chupacabras yawning, shuddering and growling awake.

Worse, the compounded odor of so many Chupacabras in such a concentrated space was paralyzing. I mean this literally, as in Sarai and I were locked in place, frozen and unable to form a cogent thought.

You will probably be assuming, based on the Bigfoot vs. Chupacabra fracas at the onset of this narrative, that Chupacabras are not the friendliest of people under normal circumstances. It would logically follow that when they perceive a direct threat to their home, they are liable to be pretty grumpy about it.

So when the entire vibrating, growling, salivating mass of Chupacabra started pouring down from the branches to mob us in a smothering, stinky cocoon, I should not have been surprised.

I wish I could say this was the case, for had I been prepared, there were many things I could have done. Instead I merely opened my mouth and screamed.

CHAPTER 16

The one positive point of my un-calculated reaction is that a Yeti scream is nothing like a normal scream. In the first place, we Yeti practice meditation our entire lives, and thus rarely face a situation in which our calm demeanor is broken. By rarely I mean that many Yeti, in their long lives stretching hundreds of years, will never scream.

Clearly this is not the category I am in, and thus my reaction was troubling to some degree, in that it exhibited clearly that my demeanor, conduct, and meditative ability were not quite at the level I had believed them to be.

But back to the positive point which is that a Yeti scream is a terrifying thing indeed, even more arresting than the smell of a treeful of Chupacabras. This is because a Yeti scream is more than a mere auditory phenomenon.

A Yeti scream is a piercing, shattering, sinew-quivering wail. A Yeti scream covers the full spectrum of sound from the subsonic to the ultra-sonic. A Yeti scream makes your skin tingle and your hair stand up on end. A Yeti scream is a vehicle for all the deeply buried fear and pain a Yeti spends their entire life trying to master through good conduct and meditation. A Yeti scream is as much a psychic wave as an auditory one.

The second aspect of the Yeti scream comes from the fact that Yeti also have very big lungs. Thus the scream, which has the side-effect of paralyzing the screamer nearly as much as the listeners, can last several minutes because the screamer has no way to shut it off.

Picture if you can the tableau we made: hundreds of slavering Chupacabras with bared fangs, gleaming red eyes, frozen in attack, surrounding a seven-foot tall Yeti with his mouth wide open in the shape of a howl.

I was glad Sarai was behind me, not only because it positioned me as a barrier between her and the Chupacabras, but also because I could not see her face— while what ever look it held would be frozen there for the entire, embarrassing interval, the eyes could still convey all sorts of information. Small blessings are better than none at all.

The silver lining to the whole situation was that a couple minutes in—although still physically paralyzed and still unleashing the paralyzing wave—my mind had gained a certain sense of detachment and I was able to actually think.

Better late than never, and this turned out to be the salvation of, not only what was to immediately follow, but our entire interaction with the Chupacabras.

CHAPTER 17

In my embarrassment at being unprepared and screaming, the first thought that entered my mind was the distinct wish that I had reacted in a manner completely opposite to the way in which I actually had. For a Yeti this is not merely an abstract idea.

By this I mean to say, if I could produce a sound so powerful, so terrifying and arresting that it stops dead in their tracks all within in hearing, I could also produce a sound with the opposite effect.

I cannot tell you exactly how much time had passed before my lungs finally ran out of air and the scream faded, but suffice it to say that it was a while. Coming unstuck a good deal sooner than the others, however, I had ample time to draw in another deep breath, close my eyes and compose myself, and begin to sing.

This sound I now produced was quite the opposite of the scream. It had a rich, warm, mellifluous quality that felt on the skin like the kiss of a sunset, on the fur like the caress of the gentle zephyr wind. It penetrated deeply into the body, massaging the vital organs and filling one up with a joyful feeling. It was calming. It was inviting. It not only sounded, but felt, really good.

Not a bird in the forest was stirring. Not an insect buzzing. Neither Human, Yeti, nor Chupacabra twitched. Even the plants stopped rustling, as though poised for the next note, captivated by vibration they had no ears to hear.

I sang in the mystical Yeti language of my home. I sang of all my happy memories—a my young Yeti's wonder at new-fallen snow, of warm Yak milk fresh from my favorite Yak, of the astonishing beauty of the mountains of my birth, the brilliant rose of sunset lighting up their soaring peaks, of days spend in peaceful contemplation with my only companion the babbling brook, of long winters spent in deep, luscious sleep, of waking up to the world's rebirth with the alpine flowers blooming in the valleys, of friends and family and everything good.

At some point I lost myself completely. To put it another way—I disappeared and there was only the song.

When I returned to myself, all the Chupacabras stood around me in a circle, swaying imperceptibly, their faces bearing beatific expressions (or at least as beatific as furry fanged persons with gleaming red eyes can be.)

Just outside the circle was Sarai, appraising me with new eyes.

CHAPTER 18

"You're certainly full of surprises," said Sarai.

I had just finished my song and the Chupacabras were still slightly swaying, utterly enchanted. I supposed their lives in the forest's heart they had been never exposed to the ecstasy of a Yeti song. I felt this would be a good time to begin negotiations, but unsure of exactly how to effect this, I chose to simply sit down in the center of the circle.

As the effect of the song eventually faded, the Chupacabras began to assess this novel situation. By assess, I mean sniff, grope, peer, taste, and whatever other modes of investigation the five senses allowed.

They seemed especially interested in Sarai, never having had close exposure to a Human before, and certainly not one who was willing to stand still and submit to the sniffing, groping, peering and tasting.[10]

Before long, the pack of Chupacabras were chattering enthusiastically to each other, the appearance of two *friendly* strangers at their home tree being surely a singular event. This was advantageous, as it gave me a chance to begin to learn their language.

We Yeti are quite good with languages, having at least seventy ourselves—being extremely insular, even among own kind, and spending most of our long lives in the remotest of caves in the highest mountains, dialects do tend to arise.

Add that to a mastery of most human languages (for reasons which I will not go into now, but suffice it to say that we are watching), and the fact that almost all of these Human languages derive from our own original, itself the source of your own Indo-European proto-tongue, you end up with a facility for learning new language quickly.

If you're wondering how we can keep all of this information in our heads, I refer you simply to the larger size of our Yeti skulls.

---

[10] As you would expect, the customary Human reaction upon meeting a Chupacabra, what with the long fangs, claws and gleaming red eyes, is to scream and go running, or if armed, to open fire.

Thus, I was shortly able to begin a rudimentary dialogue, although it took several hours of patient listening to gain enough of grasp to speak more meaningfully.

During this time, many of the Chupacabras drifted off to do, I assume, Chupacabra things. They had also lost interest in Sarai, having poked, prodded, sniffed and licked her to their little hearts' content. You can probably guess what Sarai was doing—observing, sketching and taking notes to her own heart's content.

CHAPTER 19

Once the real negotiations began, the Chupacabra
chief, whose name can only be approximated in letters—
Skzzrj[gurgle][burp][11] is close enough, but I'll just call him
Skzzrjgurgle for short—went into a tirade about all the
mess we'd made of their carefully maintained forest paths.

Chupacabras being both extremely excitable and
highly detail oriented, this tirade went on for several hours.
If you've never heard Chupacabras speak, their voices are
highly modulated, high-pitched, scratchy, and they talk
very, very fast.

---

[11] I swear there was one Chupacabra who name even incorporated
a well timed fart–pronouncing that name took some practice I can
tell you!

By patient assurance, I was eventually able to get Skzzrjgurgle to concede that the damage would be erased soon enough by the natural regrowth of the forest.

I then moved the discussion on to the subject of the Bigfoots. Not unexpectedly this wiped out all of the calm I had cultivated up to that point, and Skzzrjgurgle started in on a tirade that went on for several more hours before I was able to get him settled down enough to really discuss it.

It turns out that it wasn't the Chupacabras encroaching on the Bigfoot territory, but the Bigfoots who had been encroaching on the Chupacabras' territory, specifically their feeding grounds. This had left the Chupacabras rather hungry of late, and unless you are used to fasting as we Yeti are, there are few things like an empty belly to put one in a sour mood.

From my description of the Chupacabra attack on the Bigfoots, you are probably thinking Chupacabras are vicious creatures. Nothing could be farther from the truth. Sure, when they are threatened or provoked, Chupacabras will react violently, but then there are very few creatures who will 'turn the other cheek'. It's simply a part of the survival instinct. Unprovoked, the Chupacabras are decidedly non-violent.

The name "Chupacabra" comes from the Spanish and means "goat sucker", a reference to the goats found with puncture marks and drained of blood that the Chupacabras are sometimes forced to prey on.

In fact, goats are not the natural Chupacabra food source at all. They only feed on livestock when in the direst of straits—confused, lost and crazed by starvation. Chupacabras prefer to keep a healthy distance from Humans of all stripes, hairy or no.

The Chupacabras are night hunters, moving silently through the forest canopy until they spy an unsuspecting forest deer, which is their primary food source. The Chupacabras then sneak up, and this is where the rolling in dung comes into play, the scent acting as olfactory camouflage, and latch on to the sleeping animal with their long claws that are so good for hanging. You can probably guess what happens next—they sink in their fangs and enjoy a nutritious meal of warm, fresh blood.

Since Chupacabras are much smaller than their prey, this act of feeding is decidedly non-lethal. Sarai told me about the Masai people in Africa who tap their cattle for blood for in much the same way, mixing the blood with the milk of the cow for a healthy and delicious meal. (Think of it as a warm blood smoothie.)

Chupacabra saliva also has two very interesting properties: first, that it works as a local anesthetic so their bites are painless; and second, that it has powerful anti-bacterial properties so that not only will the small puncture wounds will never get infected, but the overall health of the animal is improved.[12]

In other words, the Chupacabras live in harmony with their environment, carefully maintaining their food stocks, and leaving a light ecological footprint.

Further, the Chupacabras, like most other human species are omnivorous.

Thus when animal resources are scarce, Cabras can get by for quite a while on fruits, insects, and other forest foodstuffs.

Much of this I deduced over the course of a nine-hour tirade. If you think that's a long time to sit and listen to a Chupacabra yelling at you, I'm here to tell you it was nothing compared to the tirade that followed, sparked off by my suggestion of a truce with the Bigfoots. *That* tirade lasted close to three days!

My nearly 42 years of meditation practice really came in handy as I had to spend the entire time sitting cross-

---

[12] Some of this I intuited through my discussions with the Chupacabras, some I learned later when Sarai had a chance to analyze their saliva.

legged and motionless across from the excitable Skzzrjgurgle, who stomped around, waving his arms and shaking his furry little fists, yelling almost without interruption in his scratchy, squeaky, highly modulated voice. (At the time it struck me as almost comical and I had to be very careful lest a betray a smile.)

The Chupacabras had a long list of grievances against the Bigfoots, most of it very specific such as "ruined the patch of fungus by the mossy tree at the sharp bend of the creek", and "broke off several branches of the knotty tree by the third-best sinkhole", and on and on for nearly three days, with the bulk of the Chupacabras sitting around us, agreeing emphatically with Skzzrjgurgle, commenting, and throwing in grievances they wanted to make sure weren't glossed over or left out.

Finally, at the very end of the three-day tirade was the serious stuff. This came down to two main points: "scaring off all the forest deer" and the recent violence.

The scaring off of the forest deer was important for obvious reasons, and the recent violence referred to the several Chupacabras who had been squashed, two of whom for which I was partly responsible.

When Skzzrjgurgle finally paused, satisfied that he'd made his point, he dropped off almost instantly to sleep.

"I thought he'd never shut up." Murmured Sarai, who was snuggled up against my back, though how long she had been there I do not know. It could have been hours, it could have been minutes.

It was dusk and all the Chupacabras were snoring softly. I was exhausted myself.

Then, as night fell, the Chupacabras began to rise, drifting languidly off and in ones and twos into the dark jungle to forage and feed.

Then I spoke to Sarai as I never had before, really opening up and sharing my deepest feelings.

I told her about my loneliness at leaving home for the first time, of my fear, drifting on a raft for months, not knowing where I'd land. I spoke to her of my guilt over the death of those two Chupacabras, and how I hoped that by making peace, I could partly atone. How sometimes it all seemed so overwhelming. I do not know how long I talked, but it must have been hours.

Then I finally allowed myself to close my eyes.

CHAPTER 20

I have no idea how long I was out, but when I cracked my eyes open, it was daylight and I was at the center of a pile of a hundred or so sleeping Chupacabras. Sarai was grinning at me, sitting on a log a little ways off, putting the finishing touches on a drawing.

I was going to need a bath.

The one fortunate aspect of Chupacabra stink is that, after a few days of exposure, your nose becomes numb. It takes a lot of incentive, though, to get to that point. Being partly responsible for two deaths and hoping to atone was powerful incentive for me; for Sarai, getting the improbable opportunity to observe a previously unrecorded human species was, as ever, more than enough.

What I really wanted was to get up and stretch, having been seated and largely unmoving for more than four days, but I didn't want to wake the gently rising and falling pile softly snoring Chupacabras.

After all, I've sat in meditation for months at a time, this being part of every Yeti's training, although it was always in nice, sub-zero caverns where it's much easier to slow the metabolism.

At any rate, despite the warmer clime, I could go a bit longer and I figured the Chupacabras would start waking up around sunset anyway, which was not long off.

The situation did give me time to think and formulate a strategy. I needed some way to defuse the hostility between the Chupacabras and the Bigfoots, but being a stranger in the region, I had no idea if such an outcome could be effected.

How wrong had been my initial assumptions about the Chupacabras! Not that my response was not natural. After all, they did tend to have a bit of a vicious look about them, what with their gleaming red eyes and prominent fangs. Add to that the arresting odor and the fact that my first experience of them was as attackers.

Yet, having now gotten to know them, I now could see them as the slightly crabby, but overall friendly folks they were when not being threatened.

Contrast this with the Bigfoots, much closer evolutionary cousins of Yeti. This physical similarity had led me to take Frrbrgr's part of without ever thinking—a snap judgment I could now see was flawed.

In actuality the Bigfoots, in my short time interacting with them, had proven to be aggressive, violent and not entirely honest.

I was pretty sure I could get the Chupacabras to accept a reasonable compromise if such a compromise could be found, but what about the Bigfoots?

That was an obstacle I'd have to deal with later. At the moment, I had a swarm of Chupacabras I needed to convince. I certainly seemed to have won them over with my magical song, and that was a start. This would surely grant me some influence in the coming negotiations.

There were two main problems the way I saw it.

First, I would have to speak for the Bigfoots, having no idea if they would accept the solution I proposed. Second, ever since the incident resulting in the deaths of the two Chupacabras which I had unwittingly caused, I was no longer blindly confident in myself—what might at first seem like the obvious solution could very well bring about other, previously unforeseen consequences.

My people have a saying, "Certain in the morning, uncertain at night. Uncertain in the morning, certain at night."[13] It had always seemed like a silly aphorism, a clever ordering of words without any real meaning. Now, tempered by experience, I could see both it's wisdom and practicality.

Yes, I was now unsure of myself, but that only meant I was aware now not only of what I knew (i.e. the facts at hand), but also that there was a lot that I *didn't* know. Understanding this at least allowed me to proceed with caution.

At this point an old Yeti story came into my head, one we tell our children at bedtime. Every Yeti knows it. It is the story of "Frak and Jak".

---

[13] In other words, if one begins from a position of certainty, but honestly analyzes their own assumptions, questions are sure to arise. But if one begins from a position of doubt, and proceeds by rigorously analyzing all the available data, one is likely to end up with some solid, fact-based conclusions. Of course I may be missing some other meaning entirely, but this interpretation worked in the context.

THE TALE OF
FRAK AND JAK

Long ago, in the time before Atlantis returned to the stars, there were two important Yetis called Frak and Jak, both with their eye on a certain piece of land.

The land in question was a hill at the center of a lovely little valley, ringed all around by majestic mountains. The mountains were of such great height that they shielded the valley from bitterest of winds, and the hundreds of waterfalls which flowed down their sides made the floor of the valley inviting and lush. The climate was temperate and the mists churned up by the crashing of waterfalls onto the rocks gave the valley a balmy feel, both exceedingly pleasant and highly picturesque. At sunrise and sunset, when the changing light interacted with the mists, the landscape took on a magical aspect—incredible hues and auspicious shapes would play across luminous sky, and no two moments were ever the same. Thus a person could gaze out across the valley and never grow tired of the sight. It was truly a kind of paradise.

To Jak, a farmer with no small herd of yaks, the hilltop was the perfect spot to build a house, for not only were the views magnificent, there was plenty of grazing in the valley below.

Frak, however, was not thinking of a house, for he was a miner by trade and a good one at that. He spent his days digging precious minerals from the mountains, and when he was not digging he was thinking about digging. It was all he ever talked about. For Frak the true value of the hill was in what lay beneath—namely, a rich vein of gold extending deep into the earth.

Both Yetis had their hearts so set on the place that a feud arose. Although nearly unknown these days in Yeti culture, back then such disputes were not at all uncommon. The disruption caused was so great that soon the neighbors were becoming involved. There was much argument and grumbling, with half the Yetis siding with Frak, and the other half siding with Jak. At one point the two sides almost came to blows! Eventually the case had to be taken before the Yeti King, lest things get truly out of hand.

The Yeti king listened to the arguments brought forth by both sides—Jak who wanted to build a home, and Frak who wanted to dig the gold. After some deliberation, the King decided that both sides had merit, for he was fond of Yak milk, and Jak's Yaks were among the finest, but he was also rather fond of gold. The conclusion of the King was that Jak would have the surface of the hill on which to build his house, while Frak would have the mineral rights to whatever lay beneath. Thus each would have what they wanted, and no one the worse for the other's gain. Both parties found the solution acceptable, and went their respective ways.

Jak immediately began to build his house, and before the first snowflake had touched upon the brittle grass, the house was complete. A truly lovely house it was, built to be cool and airy in the summer, in the winter cool and snug, and there were any number of terraces and eaves, and a central courtyard with a gurgling fountain. Everyone agreed it was a house fit for a king.

Frak however, with the whole winter to mull things over, started to believe he had been tricked.

"It's all well and fine for Jak," thought Frak, "who now has a sumptuous manor to call his home, but I have nothing out of it. Certainly I have been cheated!"

As the winter dragged on, and it was a particularly long and harsh one, Frak's bitterness grew and grew, surpassing even the bitterness of the season. Eventually he decided that as soon as the weather was good enough, he would venture forth with an armed force to kill Jak and raze his manor to the ground. Thus, he would be free to extract his gold from beneath the hill with no one to say otherwise.

But we Yeti have ever been creatures of reason, even in our primitive past, and Frak's friends raised some compelling objections to his brutal plan.

"In the first place," they said, "Jak also has many friends, and killing them won't be easy. We're sure to lose many of our own people. In the second place, if you murder him for his property, it will set a precedent. What then's to stop a Yeti in future from thinking 'That Frak has all that gold and I have none—I will kill him and take it for my own!'"

Frak had to agree that they made a convincing argument, but could see no other way to get his gold.

"What if," proposed his closest advisor, a Yeti known for exceeding cleverness, "we were to dig down *beside* the hill, and then tunnel *over* beneath it. In this way we can reach the gold that is rightfully yours, and Jak is none the worse for it."

"An excellent idea!" Frak exclaimed, and raised a toast to his clever advisor.

Soon enough the snow melted and that is exactly what they did.

"And then what happened?" Asked Sarai with knowing eyes. (At some point, tired of scribbling in her notebook, she'd sat down beside me and had the tale recounted.)

"Everything was fine until the rains came." I answered. "Then the hill collapsed, the house fell in the hole, and valley was poisoned with the runoff from the mine."

"Interesting." Quipped Sarai.

Interesting indeed, but it seemed to have no bearing on my present predicament!

I let out a sigh.

CHAPTER 21

As the dusk settled though the forest canopy, the Chupacabras began stir, yawning, stretching, and farting awake. If you've never had the experience, I can tell you it is quite a thing to have an entire swarm of Chupacabras yawning, stretching, and farting awake in a vibrating mass piled up around you.[14]

Soon enough they began drifting off into the forest in search of breakfast, apparently having forgotten all about the negotiations. While I didn't want to get between the

---

[14] Although my nose had been numb for days, and so there was no olfactory discomfort in the farting pile of Chupacabras all around me, the effect of the release of so much methane gas in such a concentrated area did have the effect of raising the core temperature of the pile by several degrees.

Cabras and their bellies, I also didn't want things to drag on too much longer, lest renewed violence break out, so I started to sing. It was just a Yeti children's song, but it had the effect I was hoping for—all the Chupacabras drifted back to settle in a circle around me.

So far, so good. Now I just had to convince them to make peace with the Bigfoots! This was going to be a tricky proposition as I had nothing to offer in return—no reparations, no guarantees.

What I arrived at was this: 1. Surely the rainforest was a big enough place for both Bigfoots and Chupacabras to live in peace; 2. If the Bigfoots were encroaching on Chupacabra territory, there must be some reason for it, and that reason should be addressed; and finally, 3. That peaceful coexistence is always preferable to war, war having the nasty tendency to result in death.

With no other real options, I took a deep breath and launched into a speech explaining all my view.

Luckily, as captain of my Yeti school debate team for several years running, this kind of thing was completely natural to me. I had some pretty impressive debate performances in my time, I can tell you, but nothing compared to the poetry, the eloquence, the sheer persuasive power of my arguments on that day.

I must have gone on for a while too, because when I stopped talking, dusk had transformed into night, and the stars were peeking in between the softly rustling leaves of the canopy above.

The Chupacabras began chattering away, speaking so quickly and raising such a great cacophony, I was not able to make much sense of what they were saying.

Fortunately, this went on for a surprisingly short time, minutes as opposed to hours or days (for if you will recall, I still had not stirred from my seated position, now well into my fifth day). Then, just as quickly as the cacophony had risen, it settled down into hushed silence. Skzzrjgurgle spoke:

Skzzrjgurgle said that in his opinion, and his opinion being the opinion of the swarm, that they saw the matter as settled. It turns out that the central tenant of Chupacabra philosophy is "do unto others as they do onto you." Thus, as long as the Bigfoots ceased their aggression, they'd have no problem from the Chupacabras.

I have to admit, this floored me. Everything I'd learned in school, of the endless histories of endless wars, that once plagued Yetis in the distant past, and still plagued Mankind to this very day, had led me to believe that making peace must be a difficult thing indeed.

In retrospect, I should not have been so surprised, based on the overall peaceful, though admittedly excitable, nature of the Chupacabras. I guess that, having gotten all their grievances off of their chests, the Chupacabras considered it 'water under the bridge'—no point in dwelling on the past.

This trait, so natural to these furry little people, was something I'd been working towards my entire life, something all Yetis work toward. In fact, 'Living in the Present" is an entire subject in Yeti school!

I reflected that if people were more like Chupacabras (perhaps not in the respect of rolling in poop and slobbering profusely, but in sense of being able to let go of the past), they would certainly lead much happier lives.

With the matter seemingly resolved, at least on the Chupacabra side of things, it was apparently time to celebrate.

The Chupacabras broke out the only artifact I have seen them use—preserved gourds. The Chupacabras were swigging from the gourds and passing them around. As you can imagine, they all wanted to pass a gourd to me, being by this time something of a celebrity among the swarm, and so I had to swig out of nearly all of them.

I didn't immediately realize that the liquid sloshing within was alcoholic!

CHAPTER 22

Thankfully I'd had some experience with alcohol. Well, one experience at any rate. Namely, my send-off party when I left the Yeti homeland to experience the world.

Reflecting on it now, I am convinced that the sendoff party—at least the alcohol part of it—is staged to teach us a lesson, as outrageous as that seems!

I had a headache for a week after the aforementioned send-off, an indicator, I am certain, of a toxic level not at all within safe parameters. In other words, alcohol poisoning. (I still get upset thinking about it, adults giving liquor to kids, even if they are 42 year-old kids. And they're supposed to be the responsible ones!)

I was so sick by the end of the sendoff that I threw up what seemed like dozens of times, even after all the contents of my stomach had long been expelled! (If you have never had the experience of vomiting bile, I urge you to avoid it at all costs.)

The remainder of that horrible night I lay there, world spinning crazily around me as I clung to the floor in an effort to stop it wishing I was dead, which should give you an indication of how great was my suffering. It was only late the next morning that the world gradually returned to standing still, or at any rate revolving at it's usual speed, that I stopped praying for death.

So thankful was I that terrible morning, when I finally managed to rehydrate, drinking gallons of ice-cold water from a pure, crystal stream, that I vowed never to touch the stuff (i.e. alcohol) again. Then I threw up some more.

I can tell you this was not the first vow I've broken, nor I'm sure will it be the last, being only human, after all. At least in the present circumstance it was for a good cause, namely cementing the accord with my new friends the Chupacabras.

I learned at some point in the evening that the liquor we were drinking was actually made of a certain type of fruit-eating beetle the Chupacabras chew and spit into the gourd. There, the enzymes in the Chupa saliva promote the fermentation of the sugary juice. I was glad I had not known this factoid at the outset of the celebration!

Even Sarai took a sip, gagged, said "It's good," and took another sip to show she was sincere. When I later told her the origin of the bugjuice she looked both bemused and disgusted.

I wish I could say my that previous experience with alcohol came in handy that night, but the bugjuice crept up on one and had quite a powerful effect–it filled one with enthusiastic feeling, leading inevitably to another swig.

The positive side was I that was filled with a warm feeling of love and camaraderie for all beings, and the evening passed in a happy blur.

Such was the feeling of communion that I embraced all of my new friends, scooping up whole bundles of squirming Chupacabras into my arms, and we danced and sang together late into the night.

Just before I fell into a pleasant sleep I may have told Sarai that I loved her.

Even though I knew that it could never be, destined as we were in this life to be born different species, nevertheless it was true. I wasn't sad, though, as I lay there smiling out to my every extremity, for the knowledge that I had something equally precious, warming me through—

she was my best friend!

CHAPTER 23

I awoke the next day with the sun shining squarely in my eyes, which is some trick I can tell you, the forest canopy being thick, and a square-shaped opening a rare thing indeed.

Once again, I had a splitting headache, was fearfully dehydrated, and on the verge of throwing up. I vowed in future, were I ever in a position where I could not politely refuse an alcoholic drink, to merely smile, sip and pretend to swallow.

I had other things on my mind, however—my mission having been accomplished with the Chupacabra swarm, it was time to be heading back to the Bigfoot village.

The Chupacabras, who all likewise had splitting headaches and were staggering around, moaning and holding their heads (pausing only to vomit—little sprays directed at the ground or, more often, at each other), nevertheless gave us a grand sendoff with many hugs and big, slobbery (and yes, slightly barfy), Chupacabra kisses.

I was just as sad to leave them as they were to see me go, but I knew I would carry a special place in my heart for Chupacabras and be sure to tell others of their noble qualities.

The return journey was not as easy as the journey there. My third-eye 'epiphany' had faded somewhat—likely the headache was crimping my mental abilities—so that while I could still make out the pathways, it took some real effort.

Eventually, Sarai started to be able to see the pathways also, which was both interesting and helpful, and it allowed me to concentrate on trying not to throw up.

Sarai, in stark contrast to my sorry self—having not had to contend with nearly every Chupacabra in the swarming offering her a gourd of sloshing bugjuice to drink from—was well rested and full of energy.

Thankfully we came to a fast, cold stream before midday and in no time were splashing about in what can only be described as sheer ecstasy. It took some work I can tell you, rinsing off all the accumulated Chupacabra residue which had actually formed a stinky crust.

I had gone from snow-white to a kind of biley yellow. Sarai, though much better off than me for not having been the center of the Chupacabra's affections—and in any case, having much less hair—was nonetheless likewise encrusted, and it took her the better part of an hour to get her locks untangled.

"I think I'm actually able to smell again," said Sarai with a radiant grin.

We ate some wild fruits that were growing by the stream, and rested for the remainder of the afternoon. I must have drunk fifteen gallons of water and my headache gradually lessened to a mere dull throb.

It was only when the sun was sinking low that we reluctantly left the clear crystal stream and set out again for the Bigfoot village. Dusk was descending as we approached. In retrospect, this was not the wisest idea, as the lessened visibility made us vulnerable to attack.

CHAPTER 24

The Bigfoots were lying in ambush in the brush alongside the path where it opened up into a small clearing, and as soon as I entered the clearing they descended on me with a howling fury.

Although unprepared mentally, my body fell into a mode of pure reaction, and I countered each Bigfoot strike automatically, sending each attacker flying back into the brush.

Sarai had the good sense to fade into the background, out of the action, which helped me in that I didn't have to worry about protecting her while simultaneously fending off a small pack of very large Bigfoots.

You may be wondering why I didn't simply use my Yeti powers to stun them all and the answer has two parts. Firstly, there was no guarantee I'd have the vocal power to disable an entire group of Bigfoots, by which I mean a pack of ten-foot tall masses of pure muscle and fur. Lot of insulation there. Secondly, while I could stun a group of Chupacabras without affecting the bigger folks, a sound wave at the frequency to stun the Bigfoots would certainly have affected Sarai and could be harmful to her much more fragile form. By this I mean heart attack, stroke, organ damage or internal hemorrhaging, all of which, in the present circumstances, would mean certain death. For it is a much easier thing to cause harm than to heal.

Likewise, if I tried a mind trick, say, of the type I'd used on the kidnappers, it was as likely as not the reactions of the Bigfoots would be to fight even more ferociously.

So it was left to fisticuffs, as I later learned the Human term is, and I'd like to say, without bragging, that I comported myself admirably, fighting the pack of Bigfoots to a standstill.

Unfortunately, Grrbrgr—being perhaps marginally more intelligent than the others and seeing that the direct attack was not working so well—had snuck up on Sarai and before I knew it, he was holding her hostage.

I do not remember all of what happened next. The moral of the story is, do not piss off an adult Yeti, even if that Yeti has only just become and adult and is still figuring a lot things out. If anything, such a Yeti is more dangerous for he lacks the emotional control of one more experienced and mature.

I glared into the eyes of the Grrbrgr as I stepped towards him. You may have guessed that a Yeti glare, like a Yeti scream, is more than meets the eye. I assure you that what I was projecting into Grrbrgr's sluggish brain was no joke. A look of fear crossed his face and he immediately forgot Sarai as stumbled back in abject terror.

I know I have said earlier that anger is a disadvantage in a fight, and usually this is the case, but there is a difference between wild rage and cold fury. I can say with some certainty it was the latter which overtook me, for my next clear memory was of standing in the middle of a pile of Bigfoots, moaning at my feet.

CHAPTER 25

Now that we had the ambush situation all cleared up and the new pack hierarchy firmly established—Grrbrgr, the previous leader having been squarely beaten by me in open combat—we could safely return to the mission and accordingly, the Bigfoot village.

This was a lot easier than I was expecting, as the other Bigfoots were now taking orders from me! I'd be lying if I said it didn't give me a little boost. Although Yeti are taught to shun pride, it is truly a difficult emotion to ignore.

The looks on the faces of the Bigfoot villagers was nothing short of astonishment as we returned, me leading Grrbrgr—still not quite reconciled to the turn of events if

the look of bewilderment on his face was any indication—
by his big, furry ear.

No sooner had I released him than Mùlululu (or was
it Lùlululu or Mulùlululu?—I still hadn't cleared up which
was which!) appeared on the scene and began yelling at
Grrbrgr in a most ferocious manner. If you think an angry
Bigfoot male is fearsome, I am here to tell you it is nothing
compared to an angry Bigfoot female!

I have already related that the Bigfoot females are
bigger than the males, but it was only now I learned that
they were also in charge. I could see now that it was gender
bias—a type of false assumption based on sex—which had
led me to take Grrbrgr as chief in the first place. I took
careful note of this, lest I repeat the mistake in future.

I have also mentioned that the male/female ratio
among Bigfoots is roughly 6:1, meaning six husbands to
each Bigfoot wife. Apparently however, some of the Bigfoot
husbands, certain I'd soon grow bored of the scrawny,
nearly hairless Sarai, and threatened by my evident
popularity with their wives, had seen fit to take measures to
eliminate a prospective rival, that prospective rival being
none other than myself.

It was also evident the Bigfoots were not long-term
thinkers, for any thoughts about my helping them to
resolve the conflict between them and the Chupacabras

had been seemingly forgotten. (Possibly they thought I had wiped out the Chupacabras and was no longer needed. Having since learned a bit about how Bigfoots operate, I would not be surprised.)

In short order the other two Bigfoot Wives had appeared and soon the whole ambush group was receiving an epic tongue-lashing.

Sarai observed this all with no little amusement, having shaken off the shock of being taken hostage fairly quickly, possibly acclimated to it per her previous experience.[15]

We thought that would be the end of it until Grrbrgr did something truly stupid—not surprising, all things considered—which was to raise his hand to strike his wife. You could see her eyes change in an instant, and if I thought she'd been scary before, that was nothing compared to now. But it was when she opened her mouth as wide as it would go that *Grrbrgr's* eyes changed— changed to abject terror far more abject than the terror my glare had inspired. For what came out of the mouth of his wife, then the other two wives, was the most bone-jarring, ear-splitting, gizzard-piercing wail I have ever had the misfortune to hear.

---

[15] One can get used to the most unlikely things, as our several day stay in the nested stink of the Chupacabra swarm had proven!

Now the Bigfoot Wail may not have the psychic properties of the Yeti Scream, but trust me when I tell you that does not make it less any powerful. Especially with all three voices forming a terrifying and discordant harmony.

In an instant all of the Bigfoots had grabbed their ears and fallen to their knees, begging the wives to stop. I was pressing my palms against my ears as hard as I could but it didn't seem to help—it was like the sound bypassed the ears and went directly to the brain. The Bigfoot children were sobbing inconsolably. Grrbrgr was clutching at his wife's knees, the perfect picture of earnest repentance. But it was only when their lungs ran out of air that the keening siren of the the Bigfoot Wives finally fell silent.

The quiet that followed was like air rushing into drowning lungs, like a glass of ice water in the middle of the desert. Not a peep came from the jungle, neither chirp of bird nor buzz of insect. It may well have been the loveliest silence I've ever heard.

Soon enough, all was forgotten, the birds once again began to sing, the insects again to buzz, and things returned to normal in the Bigfoot village. Well, normal with maybe the exception of the ambushers all slinking around looking decidedly sheepish, now and then shooting accusatory looks at Grrbrgr who looked to be having the worst week of his life.

Now that I understood the true structure of the Bigfoot society, I was able to make real progress in my peacemaking.

First off, I was now de facto head honcho, in other words, Alpha Male. Secondly, the Bigfoot females were much more reasonable than their male counterparts, this second factor possibly having something to do with their larger stature and thus slightly bigger brains, or perhaps some aspect of the mothering instinct which tends to make one more prudent on important issues such as life and death.

Whatever it was, I could feel we were on the verge of a solution.

CHAPTER 26

I related to the Bigfoot Wives the intention of the Chupacabras to forget the past and move forward in peace, provided the Bigfoots stopped their encroachment into Chupacabra territory.

It was then I learned that the root of the problem was not the Bigfoots, but Humans, who were encroaching on the Bigfoot territory! This was forcing the Bigfoots to move deeper into forest and sparking tensions between themselves and the Chupacabras, who'd previously had almost no contact.

It is an unfortunate thing that when you look across the scope of Human history, such events are all too commonplace. They almost always result in tragedy and bloodshed. One group is forced from their homes by a merciless aggressor, and flee as refugees into a neighboring country where they are often met with, at best, strained tolerance, and at worst, equal aggression from the very nation with whom they have sought sanctuary!

It should be the goal of all sentient beings to live in harmony with others, especially those less fortunate. But strained resources, along with other factors such as xenophobia, often bury these higher goals like an avalanche in the mountains coming down on a group of unsuspecting hikers.

How easily can hatred, fear, and envy overtake compassion, goodwill and fellowship.

The Bigfoot Wives were wise enough to desire peace —the conflict having not gone well for either side—but now there was the new problem of Human pressure on the Bigfoot border.

In the past, when an area was overtaken by Human development—in this case a kind way of saying, "destroy everything in sight at maximum profit"—the Bigfoots could always retreat deeper into the forest. This, unfortunately, was no longer an option, pushed up as they were against the neighboring Chupacabras.

We spoke late into the night of how things had changed for the Bigfoots in recent years. I tried to look at it from every angle, but in the end, there was no getting around it. Humans were the source of problem, and it was they who must be dealt with.

My sleep that night was fitful and I made sure Sarai slept snuggled against me, lest any disgruntled Bigfoots got any stupid ideas. Still, I awoke many times, panting and twitching from supposed attacks that turned out each time to be only phantoms haunting my troubled dreams.

CHAPTER 27

The next day as we hiked out of the rainforest, Sarai and I began to formulate a plan. The mutual benefits of our partnership were soon evident in this regard—Sarai provided me with a guide for the Human world, just as I provided her guide to the hidden world.

Sarai filled me in on the history of the country, how the rainforests all over the region were being developed, often at an alarming rate. Luckily, this country was less economically advanced, which meant the rate of deforestation was relatively slow.

Sarai was surprised it was happening here because the country we were in actually had a fairly good environmental record. For this reason, we decided it might be worthwhile to investigate the situation before taking any action.

Sarai had spent some time in the capital and was familiar with the department that handled natural resources.

The trick was getting me in and out of the capital without causing a stir. Luckily, Yeti have very good camouflaging skills. These skills are so good, in fact, that legends say we can become invisible. Now I'm not saying whether this is true or not, but if it were, it would be a difficult trick, involving the bending of light, and at any rate, beyond my capabilities.

There is another explanation that is much simpler: in the high mountains above the treeline, there is snow all year around, thus a person with snow-white fur can easily fade into the background. Unfortunately, this was not our present circumstance.

However, there are certain basic camouflaging techniques all Yeti are taught before we embark on our Rumspringa journeys.

The key element that makes it easy to pass unnoticed in the Human world is how self-absorbed most Humans tend to be. A majority spend their lives driven by the pain of the past and consumed by worry about the future—in other words, not living in the present. Add to that all of the readily available distractions which they can focus on to gain some relief from the weight of past and future. This tendency has increased exponentially in the technological era by the advent of portable electronic devices, particularly smartphones and mp3 players.[16] When you combine all of these factors you have the perfect conditions for ignoring pretty much everything that's going on around you.

Even in a less developed country such as the one we were in, nearly everyone has smartphones and mp3 players, so that part of the equation was covered.

Being short for a Yeti also made the camouflage challenge somewhat easier, although there was still the problem of being covered in fur. We decided that Sarai would go in first and buy me the biggest clothes she could find.

The forest was just as thick as we approached the location where the development was supposed to begin, and I began to suspect we'd been tricked yet again.

---

[16] It's a big part of the reason "magic" has disappeared from the world—it's not that the magic is not there, just that people are so distracted they can't see it. This might be something as specific and not noticing a Yeti, or as general as not pausing for a moment of wonder at a particularly inspiring sunset which has a subtle type of magic all its own.

Then the forest abruptly stopped and what stood before us was a sea of mud and stumps as far as the eye could see. It was such a shocking shift, I completely forgot myself and just stood there, ankle deep in mud with my mouth hanging open.

"Yup," said Sarai, and left it at that.

CHAPTER 28

Seeing the devastation firsthand cemented my conviction this development must be stopped, and I spent many hours contemplating this while Sarai set off to find me some clothing.

Certainly there were economic pressures that had led to such spectacular deforestation, but there had to be alternatives. Sarai had mentioned many times that the rainforests were turning out to be a treasure trove of medicinal compounds, thus could surely yield benefits beyond simple wood.

Many parts of the world had been transformed in this way—regions once covered with lush forests turned first into cropland, then into deserts. The American Dustbowl of the 1930's is a famous recent example, a man-made ecological disaster with profound repercussions. But this phenomenon has been going on for a lot longer than that.

Perhaps the most famous ancient example is the area known as the "Fertile Crescent" where Human civilization is said to have first taken hold. It started out as a lush Eden, but slowly, over the course of countless generations, the entire region became arid and barren. Today it is mostly desert.

This agricultural transformation had surely led to the rise of Human civilization, a boon to be sure, but now with so many billions inhabiting the planet, the balance maintained for eons by nature was slowly tipping.

While this may itself be part of the natural process (i.e. evolving to the point of global impact, then going extinct), as sentient beings we can apply our intelligence toward addressing the matter.

Yet intelligence is no guarantee of success. Even we Yeti, by all accounts a highly intelligent and civilized species, brought this world to the brink of destruction. Our pride at our technology and certainty of our infallibility led to the end of the last Ice Age—commonly known as the Holocene period—when the glaciers retreated from most of the the planet. Our reckless behavior and wanton "progress" transformed the earth from a frosty Yeti paradise to much warmer, wetter place, a paradise not for Yetis but for Man. By all accounts we were lucky to have survived this transformation, withdrawing to our mountain retreats while Humans boldly inherited the earth.

How many intelligent species have been brought down by their own success on how many planets I cannot say, but Atlantean legends make them countless, the universe being a very big place. No one knows the future, not even Yeti, but Humans are going to have to change a good many habits if they expect the planet to remain hospitable for their own future generations!

The depressing vista over which I now gazed was being stripped of wood and would likely be turned into pasture for cattle. Those who are passionately against this type of transformation argue that the forests are the world's lungs, recycling carbon from the atmosphere, without which the earth's environment will spin out of control. This is a subject of some study and every year scientists learn more and more—discount their finding at your own peril!

In the present case however, it wasn't a matter of science, but of immediate harm—the deforestation was directly impacting the population which depended on the forest for survival, specifically the Bigfoots and Chupacabras.

These weighty matters occupied my mind as I sat on the verge of destruction that was the border between the forest and the sea of stumps. I was actually starting to get a little depressed, but fortunately, before the gloom could take hold, Sarai returned.

She had with her a large and intricately woven garment called a 'poncho'. A poncho is essentially like a blanket, in this case a very big blanket, with a hole for one's head to go through. Sarai related that it actually had been a huge blanket that the vendor had turned into a custom garment on the spot, there not being many seven-foot people in the region. In any case, it had the effect of covering my body from shoulders to toes, which was exactly what was needed, and to top it all off, she had also brought me a hat with a very broad brim, perfect for covering most of my face.

The rest of the camouflage would rely on my body language, specifically projecting an aura that makes me less noticeable to the casual observer.

You might suppose this is some kind of magic power but I assure you it is not. In fact, many humans have mastered this skill, usually very shy people who prefer to blend into the background, but also secret agents whose very lives often depend on passing unnoticed among a foreign populace.

Sarai'd had the good idea to hire a driver, a friendly man with a pickup truck who didn't look at me too closely or ask any questions. (Truth be told, he seemed to much prefer looking at Sarai, and Sarai didn't seem to mind.)

I had time to analyze my feelings on this, riding in the back of the pickup for several hours as we wended our way into the capitol. I ultimately decided that anything which facilitated our important mission, even the enthusiastic attentions of a stranger towards my friend and companion, must be a blessing. In other words, any Human interest in Sarai per her womanly attributes was another valuable layer of concealment. And while I can see now that the way Sarai chatted up the driver for almost the entire ride, making him grin and even sometimes blush, was surely designed to keep him from thinking about the mysterious giant in the back of his truck, I'd be lying if I said that at the time it didn't bother me a little bit.

I definitely attracted some attention as we drove through the mud streets of the shantytowns at the outskirts of the city. A shantytown, if you've never seen one, is essentially a community made up of poorly-constructed, ramshackle huts. The people there, being too poor to afford many distractions, tended to see what was in front of them much more clearly.

However, I was apparently not such a strange sight as to cause much of a stir, except among the children, who see things very clearly indeed, but are too small to be taken seriously. I even grinned and waved at one little barefoot girl who, jaw dropped, stood in dirt of the roadside while we idled, waiting for a train to pass.

CHAPTER 29

The deeper we got into the city, the less notice people took of the giant hunched in the back of the beat-up old pickup truck.

I was, of course, trying to remain as inconspicuous as possible, but I had never been in a Human city before, and every new sight and sound was compelling. I could not help but peek out from under my broad-brimmed hat, more than was probably prudent.[17]

---

[17] Although Yeti do have a city, it is mostly underground, and the above-ground portion is designed in a way so that unless you really knew what to look for, you wouldn't think it was a city all. Architecture like that is not an easy thing to pull off, but of course, we've had tens of thousands of years to develop it.

At one point we got stuck in a traffic jam and I became very nervous lest some bored driver should scrutinize me closely. However all of the drivers seemed more interested in the cause of the traffic jam, which turned out to be a large group of workers marching with signs. They were protesting long hours and unsafe conditions in the city's many factories.

As the protesters passed us by, flowing between the idling cars, one particularly enthusiastic marcher looked right at me and raised his fist defiantly in the air, a gesture, I later learned, of worker solidarity. He had to have seen a good part of my furry face, but possibly took it to be the big white beard of an elderly man, for he did not pause or look at all shocked.

It took a while to get free of the traffic jam, even after the marchers had passed, but once we were finally clear, we made the Ministry in no time.

Sarai arranged for the driver to wait for our return, and he was only too happy to oblige. I could feel his eyes glued to Sarai as we walked up the steps to the entrance of the Ministry—again fortunate, despite my discomfort, in that he never so much as glanced at me.

There were plenty of people around, but as expected, they were so completely absorbed with their smartphones that they were oblivious to each other, much less the unlikely pair headed up the Ministry steps.

The guard at the registration desk didn't even bother to glance up from the soccer match he was watching as we signed in, which I was glad for, even as a part of me was bothered that he took his duties so lightly.

The office of the Minister of the Interior, that's the public official in charge of land and natural resources, was on the 5th floor. Although Sarai was sure we'd never get in to see him, she figured we could at least corner some Undersecretary and try to shake him down (her words) for information.

I was confident however that I would be able to get us through the door to the Minister's office—in cases like this it's always better to go straight to the top, and "where there's a will" as they say.

I felt the stairs would be the safest route, but Sarai had a much different take:

"Nobody ever looks at anybody in an elevator." She said. "It's one of the perpetually awkward situations of modern society."

Sarai related that the stairs were used almost exclusively by the healthiest people who have a lot more energy to notice things.

"If we bump into one of them on their way down, there's no telling what could happen." Sarai said.

I was skeptical but I trusted her, this being her world after all, although I grabbed a thick sheaf of discarded newspapers with which to cover my face, should the need arise. However my concerns were quickly allayed as Sarai's thesis proved to be correct.

While we were the only ones on the elevator at first, several people got on at the second floor, and as predicted, no one gave us so much as a glance. In fact, as I peered at the people over the edge of my newspapers, they seemed to especially avoid looking at me!

The people in question were all overweight and seemed tired just to be standing. It wasn't hard to see why they were overweight either—many of them took the elevator up just a single floor!

Sarai says most Humans today have a far too sedentary lifestyle—a fancy way of saying they sit around all day on their butts. All I can say about it is if you ever have the choice between taking the elevator and the stairs, choose stairs!

We got off at the fifth floor where the people waiting for the elevator stepped back to let us exit, not even glancing in my direction (although the men definitely took a good look at Sarai—she was continuing to work extremely well as a portable distraction.)

"Let's at least try the Minister." I said to Sarai.

She looked skeptical but led the way.

We entered into a kind of front office, much nicer than the hallways which were actually sort of dingy. As soon as we entered, the Minister's secretary, without looking up, announced that the Minister wasn't taking any appointments for the rest of the afternoon.

Sarai made a sound somewhere between a sigh and a snort and started to leave, but when she saw I wasn't going anywhere, she also stayed put.

"I really am sorry," said the secretary, looking neither sorry, nor up from her computer. "But the Minister is completely booked."

Instead of leaving I took off my big hat and cleared my throat with the deepest, most impressive rumble I could manage. Finally the secretary looked up. Her eyes widened and her jaw dropped, and for a moment I saw in her face the face of the little girl in the dirt of the roadside.

"We'll see the Minister now, if that's alright." I said in my most persuasive and civilized voice.

The secretary just nodded dumbly and we walked past her into the inner office.

CHAPTER 30

Now you're probably thinking I used some kind of Yeti mind trick on the secretary but that wasn't the case—simple human psychology was all that was needed.

When confronted with something out of their normal range of experience, most people are unable to form a response. Think of a computer crashing because it 'cannot compute.'

I was quite far out of the secretary's realm of experience as I had suspected I would be, and confronted with a seven foot tall Yeti in a poncho she had no response. This rendered her effectively neutral, unable to fulfill her primary function, which was evidently to keep people from bothering the Minister.

I say this because the Minister was fast asleep in his chair, feet up on his desk, snoring away with a blissful expression on his face.

I sat down in one of the chairs facing his desk and dusted off my hat. Sarai plopped down beside me.

"Are you just going to let him sleep?" she whispered.

"It'll have more impact if he wakes up on his own." I whispered back.

"Aren't you worried about security showing up?" she whispered.

If you're thinking I was playing things rather cooly after revealing myself to the secretary, I'll tell you why I wasn't worried.

Put yourself in the secretary's position. What would you sound like on the phone to security, telling them an imaginary creature had just barged into the Minister's office? At best they'd think you were pulling a prank, at worst they'd drag you away to a padded room somewhere.[18]

No, unless there were the sounds of a struggle coming from the Minister's office, the secretary was unlikely to take any action.

---

[18] i.e. the "funny farm", "loony bin", "booby-hatch", and "nuthouse".

All of this I related to Sarai, and as she was mulling it over, the Minister started to stir. He snorted, stretched out his arms and peeped open his eyes. Then his eyes nearly popped out of his head. Well, one of them actually did pop out—we later learned it was a glass eye.

The Minister was so astonished to find a seven-foot tall Yeti in a poncho sitting across from him that he completely forgot all about his wayward eye, which was rolling across his desk in our direction. The glass eye dropped to the floor and the Minister began to sputter incoherently, seemingly unable to form a meaningful sentence.

We were in no hurry, so Sarai and I sat and waited to see what he would finally settle on.

"Impossible. Impossible" sputtered the Minister.

Sarai raised an eyebrow and looked at me. I winked.

"I'm not to have any meetings today. It's simply impossible. I was quite clear about that with my secretary," said the Minister, fumbling for the phone and calling his secretary, which we knew because we could hear the phone ringing in the outer office.

The Minister engaged in a hushed, urgent conversation, mainly having to do with him having important work and not having time for interruptions.

The question of calling security came up, but the Minister eyed us and evidently decided that if I hadn't eaten him by this point, the diplomatic approach might be best.

It helped that I had located his wayward eyeball and presented it to him as a token of our goodwill. It helped even more that I did it without using my hands. And no, I don't mean that I used my feet. What I used was my mind. (More on this later.)

The Minister slowly returned the phone to its cradle, his real eye fixed on the his other eye, the glass one, which was floating in front of him not two inches from his face.

CHAPTER 31

"Well, of course, it's absolutely illegal," said the Minister.

We'd filled him in on why we were here without going into too many details. In other words, we made it all about the environmental impact, without mentioning Bigfoots or Chupacabras (although with me sitting there in front of him in his office, he had to suspect there was more than met the eye, whether glass or actual).

"No development can be undertaken without going through this office. The laws are very clear on that," said the Minister.

"Well, it's happening," said Sarai, narrowing her eyes, "The question is, what are you going to do about it?"

"I wish it were that simple," replied the Minister. "You see, it's quite a different thing, *having* a law and *enforcing* a law."

"Then what's the point of having the law in the first place!" retorted Sarai.

"In a perfect world..." the Minister began.

"Clearly it's not perfect," Sarai snorted.

"In a perfect world," the Minister continued, "such violations would be easy to stop. But as you note, this is not the case. I could levy a fine, certainly, but then the company would take us to court. Even if they couldn't win the case, it would tie us up for years and drain my department's already strained resources. By the time it was all finally settled, the damage would be done."

"At least you'd be doing something," said Sarai. "Surely that's better than throwing up your hands and saying there's nothing to be done!"

Sarai was getting rather exasperated with the Minister's matter-of-fact take on things.

"Quite the contrary, my dear," replied the Minister. "It's rare for a company to take actions which require substantial investment, illegal actions especially, without the certainty there will be returns on that investment."

Sarai was about to make a retort, but the Minister, pausing for a moment from polishing his glass eye, held up a finger to silence her.

"Even ignoring the fact that any fines levied would likely be far less than the profits accrued," continued the Minister, "that a company would undertake such action in the first place implies political connections. Whoever is undertaking the present, illegal development, surely has such connections and all the requisite assurances."

"Aren't you even going to try find out who's behind it?" sputtered Sarai in disbelief.

"It's better if I don't know," replied the Minister. "Most likely it's the President's brother, and if he finds out I've been mucking about in his business it will very likely cost me my job, and probably my pension, which would be even worse. And imagine who they'd then bring in to replace me. Someone who wouldn't go making waves, I assure you."

"But there are lives at stake!" burst Sarai.

"My dear, there are always lives at stake," replied the Minister, "And still we must get on with the day to day."

"It doesn't seem like you're getting on with anything," muttered Sarai.

"As I say, my hands are tied," said the Minister, popping his glass eye back neatly into its socket.

CHAPTER 32

Up until the point in the story with the levitation of the glass eye, I'd been avoiding using what would commonly be understood as psychic powers.

There are very good reasons for this, not least of which is that such powers are not to be used lightly or too often, lest the practitioner become addicted to their use. It's a major hazard in Yeti culture.

At first it seems great, that everything physical can be done by telekinesis, the practice of moving objects with the mind. One literally doesn't have to lift a finger. But as new pathways form in the brain and old ones fade, one actually starts losing the ability *to* lift a finger.

Instead of talking, one communicates by telepathy, which has the tendency to put other people out of sorts, as it is an extremely intrusive form of communication, having someone inside your mind. So everyone starts shunning that person and blocking them out. Throwing up a psychic shield is a lot easier than you might think.

Left with no external stimulus, the psychic addict, having long ceased to have any reason to leave their domicile, becomes completely isolated and turns inward to a world of their own creation.

This generally leads to madness and self-destruction and there are many hidden caves with the bones of those poor creatures who took this route and wasted away.

In the present situation however I felt a judicious use of such powers was warranted, being as they were, in the service of the greater good.

Thus I reached out with my mind to look into the mind of the Minister.

It was interesting to note that his seemingly unfazed reaction to the appearance of a Yeti in his office was due to the impression that Yetis were outside of his jurisdiction. In other words, I didn't factor into his mental math, and thus my exotic genus was irrelevant. In fact it seemed that anything not affecting his pension took up very little space in his mind, which was mostly comprised with dreams of retiring to a little orchard up in hills, to spend his days in the sunshine, reading Petrarch and Ovid and keeping bees.

It was a nice vision and gave me a little smile. I hoped for his sake he fared better than Jak!

Unfortunately, everything he was saying about the development of the land was quite correct, even his point that making waves would lead to an worse situation with a new Minister.

This wasn't mere speculation on his part either, rather a pattern of behavior in his government, which although somewhat better than other governments in the region, clearly still had problems.

Don't get me wrong—even the most advanced nations have problems of this type, the influence of money and power all too often winning out over common sense and the common good. Often but not always. In a small, developing nation like this one though, the common good barely stood a chance.

Certainly if we had had time, a scope of years, say, to address the issue, we could have worked to effect some change. Create new initiatives, stage protests, bring international pressure to bear. But we didn't have time. We needed to stop the development before hostilities were rekindled between the Bigfoots and the Chupacabras, for this was almost certain to lead to more deaths and maimings.

It seemed that somewhat more direct action would be necessary.

CHAPTER 33

The hardest part of the plan was getting Sarai to stay at the Bigfoot village instead of accompanying me to the worksite where the illegal development was taking place.

"You gotta be kidding me!" Sarai exclaimed. "You'd better think again if you think you're leaving me behind."

Once I explained my plan however, she saw the wisdom in it.

I also felt it would be safe enough to leave her in the Bigfoot village since the Bigfoot Wives had sort of taken her under their wing. Possibly they were intrigued that such a scrawny and hairless creature as Sarai had landed such a stylish and exotic 'husband' as myself, and wanted to learn her secret.

Whatever the reason, they were getting on swimmingly, and when I left the village the Bigfoot Wives were arranging Sarai's hair to give it more volume, getting it to stand up on her head using a crazy tangle of sticks and mud.

I even saw Lùlululu (although it may have been Mùlululu or Mulùlululu—I still had no way of knowing who was who because every time I'd try to straighten it out they'd just start giggling) plucking a an insect out of Sarai's hair and munching it with relish, which is the surest sign of acceptance in this Bigfoot society.

All good on that front. You must now be wondering about my plan.

A great Yeti strategist once said 'the perfect battle is the one which is never fought.' In other words, it's much better to resolve things without coming to blows.

Humans of all stripes, whether hairy or hairless, are superstitions by nature. When confronted with anomalous events, they will immediately leap to conclusions, and it's pretty much a guarantee they will usually leap to the wrong ones.

I also had the advantage of an old Atlantean concept "Feldron's Paring Blade"[19] (known to Humans as Occam's Razor), namely that when choosing between competing hypotheses, the most simple solution will nearly always be correct.

Now, if the Humans in question were to have all the facts, namely that a mythical Yeti with certain abilities was lurking in the forest and causing problems, this would be the simplest solution. Lacking that information, the conclusions they would come to were certain to be other than a mythical Yeti with certain abilities that was lurking in the forest and causing problems.

Now I could have, for instance, used my psychic powers to create *tulpa*, a kind of thought-form that you might understand as a sort of hologram. Ghostly shapes, for instance, accompanied by terrifying screams from the jungle.

This would likely have made folks assume the site was cursed, an assumption that would in turn make the more superstitious workers not want to work there, and thus make operations far more difficult.

---

[19] Also pronounced "Veldron's" depending on the dialect. As I've mentioned, we Yeti have quite a few. The F is more the Southern Yeti style, the V more Northern. There's also a variant known as "Waldron's Chopping Axe", but it is generally considered archaic.

However, such a scheme was problematic in that there would inevitably be doubters. These doubters would no doubt want to investigate, and even believing the site to be cursed or haunted, might take actions such as an exorcism, which although it wouldn't work, would be used to induce workers back to the site. This would necessitate my remaining in the area indefinitely to recreate the hauntings and re-scare the workers.

Certainly it was my aim to solve the Bigfoot-Chupacabra problem, and so too expiate for at least some of my guilt in the two Chupacabra deaths, but I was supposed to be traveling around and seeing the world, not stuck in one place for who knows how long, putting on a lightshow every night.

There are things, however, that scare humans more than ghosts.

CHAPTER 34

You may be thinking to yourself, 'What could people possibly fear more than ghosts?' Believe me, there are a few things.

Nuclear war used to be one of those things, a highly rational fear, as such a conflict could end human life on the planet. It's actually more scary to us Yeti now that Humans are no longer nervous about this possibility, the logic being that with the great Cold War over, the threat of such an event is no longer present. This is not rational, as there still exist enough nuclear missiles to bring about the extinction of nearly all life on earth, both Human and Yeti.

Terrorism seems to be what Humans have decided recently to fear most, a factor that has allowed their rulers to slowly erode their freedoms without actually doing anything to address the root causes, which nearly always have to do with profound inequity, in other words, extreme unfairness. This inequity, institutionalized over generations, creates a feeling of powerlessness, which in turn can lead confused individuals to commit horrific acts of violence. The biggest irony is that the terrorists, who *never* win, only end up bringing even more death, destruction and misery on the very people they claim to be fighting for. Talk about losing propositions!

Human history is rife with such examples. In the conflagration you call World War Two, German scientists invented rockets to launch against the British Isles. These "V" or "Vengeance" rockets, which were unguided and could land pretty much anywhere in a general area, would not have much effect in diminishing British military strength. Instead they were used against population centers, London in particular, as weapons of terror. Thousands of civilians were killed and injured.

For their trouble, the Germans had their cities firebombed, a destruction far more thorough than their own rocket strikes. The British did this not for any great strategic reason, but as an act of revenge. Thus, while I was looking for a way to discourage Humans from destroying the Bigfoot land, I did not want to do it in a way that would cause them to firebomb the whole area.

The fear I thought would be most efficacious in the current situation was one embedded in the minds of humans from earliest the dawn of civilization, when people began living together in greater and things like sanitation started to become issues. This is the fear of disease.

Probably the most famous disease is Bubonic Plague, aka "The Black Death", spread by the common rat-flea. In the Middle Ages it wiped out as much as 60% of Europe's population, and still hangs on today in the world's poorest places.

(Sarai says the overuse of antibiotics in modern medicine may well create an antibiotic-resistant "superbug" that could kill billions—*don't say you weren't warned!*)

Now I want to make clear that I did not wish to harm anybody's heath—that would be an act of violence and morally indefensible. But a little 'dis-ease', in the sense of physical discomfort, might be just the thing.

As you well know by now, we Yeti have advanced sonic abilities. I can generate sounds to stun, terrify, or fill with bliss. I can even make a sound that lifts the forest fleas from my fur without doing them any harm. Sound at different frequencies can have all kinds of effects, and the sound I was thinking of now would have a more tangible effect. By tangible, I mean with a result that is 'material' in nature.

There are certain frequencies that are felt, not heard. These are known as "subsonic" frequencies from the Latin 'sub' for beneath, and 'sonus' for sound. By felt in this case I was meaning specifically in the lower part of the digestive tract.

What I am angling at here is that the tone I employed that morning at the worksite, with all the workers just getting started for the day, was a tone that caused them, all at once, to lose control of their bowels.

Yep. I made them crap their pants.

CHAPTER 35

Don't think I am bragging. I am not proud of what I did. I am just relating what happened. Obviously this was the reason I didn't want Sarai come, the subsonic frequency being calibrated precisely to the human digestive tract.[20]

If you are wondering how I had come to know of this particular frequency, it is a tone all Yeti are aware of, the proper use of which is to ease the suffering of very old Yeti when their "pipeworks become clogged", if you know what I mean. Invariably, when young Yeti come to learn of the

---

[20] The correct tone is right around 4 Hertz, which is a measurement of frequency defined as the number of cycles per second in a periodic phenomenon. For obvious reasons I will not reveal the exact "tone", which is subtle and actually a range of frequencies, which without many generations of testing and refinement would be very difficult indeed to find. .

tone, their very first thought is to try it out on a friend. This can get messy and has led to quite a few unfortunate incidents. I am not saying whether or not I was involved in any such incidents, but only that luckily most Yeti rather quickly grow out of this phase. Strange, the types things that can become unexpectedly useful.

I could tell that the subsonic burst had worked because all work on the site came to an immediate halt. Bulldozers stopped dozing, chainsaws went quiet, even the foremen with their maps completely forgot about what they were doing. And then, as one, they all hobbled off, presumably to go clean up.

I trailed the workers, keeping to the cover of the forest, and saw that they went to a nearby stream, stripping down and washing themselves and their clothes.

There was a lot of nervous chatter going on. The simplest explanation for the mass pant-messing was sure to be an outbreak of cholera, a disease endemic to the warmer regions of the planet that causes uncontrollable, fatal diarrhoea.

Needless to say, all work ceased for the day.

CHAPTER 36

When I returned from my mission, it was clear that Sarai, with the ministrations of the Bigfoot Wives, had become something of a celebrity in the Bigfoot village.

Her hair had transformed into a two-foot high nest atop her head, and she was teaching the Bigfoot children a game she later told me was called 'kickball' (thankfully using gourds for the ball instead of a dead raccoon.)

I told her about how things had gone at the worksite and she nodded.

"If they think there's a cholera outbreak," Sarai said, "They'll have to quarantine the site and shut everything down."

The next day however, work resumed as normal! The only explanation was that the company behind the development, most likely run by the President's brother, had covered up what had happened the previous day.

Again, I put a halt to the work with a well timed subsonic burst, and again the workers hobbled off to the stream, nervously chattering. But the very next day work had started up again. The big difference now was that the workers looked distinctly unhappy to be at the site.

When the third mass evacuation happened, the workers were no longer nervously chattering, but angrily grumbling.

I even heard some talking about how the bosses didn't care if the workers got sick and died, and only cared about getting richer, and that something should be done about it.

This was the cue I was waiting for, and I returned to the Bigfoot village to prepare.

CHAPTER 37

I want to state for the record that I am in no way condoning vandalism, but in this particular case we had established that: A. the development was illegal; B. the government planned to do nothing about it; and, most importantly C. that lives would be lost if the development was not stopped.

Since what we were doing was also illegal, if we were caught there would be real consequences, such a going to jail. For this reason especially I recommend not committing acts of vandalism. (Again, for the record, I state this was an extraordinary case!)

The operation at hand was not overly complicated, so I didn't think there'd be much problem if I planned well and we were careful.

The first part of the plan was to approach the worksite in the dead of night with a cadre of Bigfoots. This was easy now that I was the 'Alpha' and they would do almost anything I told them.

There was a Human Security Guard at the site, but he was easily taken care of with a mild sonic burst. As the guard hobbled off to the stream, he emitted a stream of curses I had never heard before, but that I found very interesting.[21]

As soon as the guard was out of sight, the Bigfoots, being naturally adapted for camouflage in this environment, crept out into the job site and started breaking things.

They broke into the equipment shed and snapped the blades off chainsaws. They tore off the hood of the bulldozer and ripped out the engine parts. They pushed over a big dumptruck and sent it rolling down the hill.

The Bigfoots were very enthusiastic at the opportunity to wreak destruction, and it was somewhat

---

[21] The Spanish language seems to be a particularly rich one for colorful expletives—I highly recommend learning it if you have any interest in such things.

difficult for me to get them to stop wreaking and return to the cover of the trees! You could see them in the moonlight, smashing and stomping with a terrible joy.

But Bigfoots would never have been able to remain hidden from Humans for so long if they were not canny operators, and at the first whiff of the guard returning, the Bigfoots faded into the forest, covering their tracks behind them.

As we headed back toward the Bigfoot village, we could hear the curses of the Security Guard echoing into the night.

CHAPTER 38

This is what I was betting on: with the workers grumbling and starting to get rebellious, then the worksite vandalized, the conclusion would be that the workers were responsible.

That the Security Guard had seen nothing would only make the company think he was in on it, and although the company wouldn't be able to prove anything, with the facts at hand, it was the obvious assumption.

My recent experience however had taught me that what may at first appear to be a solution could quickly lead to new problems, specifically of the unforeseen variety.

I didn't want our act of vandalism to result in action being taken against the innocent workers. However, on the drive back from the capital I had taken the opportunity to read the newspapers I'd grabbed at the Ministry, and I derived some useful facts.

The country we were in, having problems of great iniquity between the wealthy 1% and the rest of the population, had been experiencing a period of minor social unrest. By social unrest I mean specifically that workers all over the country were pretty unhappy that they seemed to be getting poorer while their leaders were getting richer and richer, and by minor I mean that there was talk about riots and strikes, but so far, aside from a few demonstrations like the one that had caused the traffic jam in the capital, nothing major had occurred. The point is that the leaders of the country were engaged in a balancing act, not wanting to stop enriching themselves at the expense of the workers, but also not wanting to push so hard that the workers erupted into open rebellion.

For there is nothing worse for business, especially in a country such as this which depended heavily on foreign investment, than open rebellion. My hope was that the company would decide that continued development of the Bigfoot land was not worth the trouble.

The next day, when no one showed up to work, I was confident my hope had been realized. What I didn't foresee was the Man in the Suit walking into the jungle.

CHAPTER 39

The Man in the Suit was having a hard time navigating the forest underbrush. It wasn't surprising as he did not have right shoes for the job, clad in leather loafers as opposed to sturdy hiking boots. On top of that, he had a briefcase to manage which was rather unwieldy on the uneven forest floor. I had to give him credit for tenacity, though.

Of all of the responses to the sabotage, this was one I had not foreseen.

After some quick calculation I decided it would best to nip it in the bud and so I waited in a clearing for the Man in the Suit.

He stepped into the clearing and immediately froze. For what he saw was not a 7-foot tall, snow-white Yeti, but a terrifying, seventy-foot-tall forest monster glaring down at him.

You may once again be thinking this was the same kind of mind trick I used when I rescued Sarai from the kidnappers, where each of them saw their deepest fears, but again I couldn't depend on that in this situation. For all I knew, his deepest fear would be failing his mission and getting fired, which would only strengthen his resolve.

Instead, what I was doing was a mental projection, the 'tulpa' thought-form I mentioned previously, which is sort of like a hologram.

Using this method, I was able to choose what the projection looked like, and I made as fearsome as I could imagine. The result was a giant, terrifying guardian deity, sort of a walking tree with dozens of arms, jagged wooden claws, ten sets of glowing red eyes, and for a finishing touch, a set of Chupacabra fangs ten-feet long.

The ground rumbled as the projection spoke:

"YOU HAVE VIOLATED THE SANCTITY OF THE FOREST!" boomed the monster.

"I- I- I-" stuttered the Man in the Suit.

"YOU HAVE VIOLATED THE SANCTITY OF THE FOREST AND WILL BRING DESTRUCTION!"

"Yes, but, er, that's—"

"YOU WILL SUFFER ANNIHILATION!"

The Man in the Suit was shaking like a leaf, but he continued. (He had pluck, I had to give him that.)

"Yes, yes, of course we'll stop! We didn't know. We— I'm sorry!" The poor man was pleading now.

Instead of an answer, the monster began stomping toward the Man in the Suit.

Tulpa projections are tricky things. All Yeti learn how to do it as part our spiritual practice, but it's nearly always used to project 'mandalas', a kind of maze-like pattern, to help us focus and reach deeper levels of meditation.

Projecting a living being is another thing entirely and is strongly discouraged. The reason for this is because these types of Tulpas very quickly get a taste for existence.

You start off controlling them but the situation doesn't last long. What begins as an illusion slowly becomes more and more real, and that was what was exactly what was happening now, only a lot quicker than I had expected.

I now realize the reason for this was because I had imbued the projection with awesome power to make sure the Man in the Suit would be properly impressed. At the time however I was taken completely by surprise, never having attempted this type of thing before.

The projection was stomping toward the Man in the Suit, evidently to crush the life out of him, just as the Bigfoot had stomped the Chupacabras!

And if I had any doubts as to the physicality of the Tulpa, these were quickly banished at the sight of the deep footprints it was leaving behind in the forest floor.

Serves him right, you may be thinking, the Man in the Suit, ripping up all the rainforest, and illegally to boot, but I am here to tell you that taking a human life is no small thing. I would be many years atoning for the Chupacabras that had been stomped partially due my actions, and having another death on my conscious was simply not an outcome I could accept.

I never knew I could run so fast, but in the blink of an eye I had crossed the clearing, scooped up the Man in the Suit, and was running toward the worksite.

CHAPTER 40

You may be wondering why I was running toward the worksite. The answer lies in basic military strategy. Ask any strategist what the most important factor in any battle is and they will invariably answer "the terrain."

Every terrain offers both advantages and disadvantages—the trick is to gain a favorable position while forcing your opponent to take an unfavorable one.

The Tulpa I had created (which now had an existence of its own and could cause untold havoc which had not been my intention) was a forest spirit. Therefore my best chance against it was to force it to face me outside of the forest.

Luckily, the Man in the Suit had not made much progress into the forest, and so we were back at the worksite in no time. I stowed the Man in the Suit behind the ruined bulldozer and told him to stay put.

He was taking everything surprisingly well and made no argument.

I jumped up on top of the Bulldozer and began to meditate.

The trees at the edge of the forest shook and soon the monster emerged. It took three earthshaking steps into the ruin and mud of the worksite and stopped.

For a long moment nothing happened. It was as if time was suspended with the whole forest poised for what would happen next.

And then it howled.

I am here to tell you that the sound emitted by the Forest Guardian was no ordinary sound.

Now, you have read about the Yeti Scream and the Bigfoot Wail, but this Forest Monster Howl was of another order entirely.

It was a sound made of pain and anguish, dredged up across many thousands of years, shaking the muddy earth with rage, as though all the devastation enacted on the forest had been rendered into waves.

Auditory waves. Psychic waves. You could feel it shaking you to the core—your body, your mind.

It ripped across the worksite with hurricane force.

It was at once the saddest sound I have ever heard, and the most frightening.

In it I saw a future of a planet, stripped of all resources, empty of life, rendered endless wasteland.

It took all of my strength to stay rooted on top of the bulldozer against the gale force of the *Howl*, against the psychic waves of rage and pain.

Had the Man in the suit not been shielded behind the ruined yellow hulk of the bulldozer, he would have likely been ripped to shreds by the debris.

It took all of my meditative skill not to break. Everything depended on what would happen next.

I cannot tell you how long the howl lasted, probably only minutes, but it seemed like hours. (Such is the nature of these kinds of things that one loses all sense of time, overwhelmed, perhaps, by the enormity of the present.)

And then, as abruptly as it had started, it stopped.

The monstrous spirit turned around and walked back into the forest. I collapsed on the roof of the bulldozer, relieved, completely spent.

For the monster had not walked into the forest, but a *projection* of the forest, identical in every way. I had made the monster powerful, but not particularly smart, and that was my salvation that day. As soon as it entered the forest projection I let it collapse, popping out of existence and taking the monster with it.

CHAPTER 41

I sat talking with the Man in the Suit for a long time.

It turned out he had been sent out by the Company to investigate what was going on, tipped off by the Minister that there was more to the story than meets the eye.

I should have guessed such a thing would occur, politics and business being such cozy bedfellows.

I cannot even ascribe bad intentions to the Minister —for all I knew, he had leaked the information to help my cause, possibly in an effort to make up for all the terrible compromises he'd been forced to make during his time in office.

Or he could have simply been looking for a payoff.

What the truth was, I shall never know, but what I did learn from the Man in the Suit was that the Company was looking to resolve the matter peacefully.

While the Company must have been fairly certain that the sabotage was not in fact caused by disgruntled workers, would the newspapers think that?

Denials by the Company would only strengthen suspicions of a cover-up, and that would certainly be the first conclusion skittish investors would jump to.

Worse, if it somehow leaked that the sabotage was caused by imaginary creatures such as Bigfoots and Yetis, the Company and the Government would lose any last vestige of credibility. The last of the stalwart investors would flee like fleas from a sinking Bigfoot.

As I'd suspected, the Company did not want even the rumors of social unrest to surface. If investors were to stop investing, or even go so far as to liquidate their assets, the economic devastation that could follow would be far worse than the devastation of our little patch of rainforest—it could bring down the economy of the entire country!

President's brother or no, the people in charge were not going to let that happen.

To them, it was a simple matter of the bottom line. In other words, dollars and sense.

It is even possible that if the real truth could be revealed, that a new species of human had been discovered.

The entire region would become off-limits for forever. This was certainly not an outcome the Company would look forward to!

Abandoning the site and letting the jungle retake it, leaving the Bigfoots in peace, was now the win-win solution for everyone involved.

Just to be sure, I once more used my psychic powers, this time to look into the Man's mind, and I saw that he was telling the truth.

It turns out that the Company and the government had always known there were Bigfoots in the region, they just didn't realize they were encroaching on their territory.

"We can leave the area undeveloped and trade for carbon credits," said the Man in the Suit, who had recovered from the ordeal surprisingly quickly. He grinned, "It's a win-win."

Of course, should good faith ever fail, there would still always be the threat of the forest monster.

You and I know it had vanished from existence, but the Man in the Suit didn't need to know that.

Win-win, indeed.

CHAPTER 42

Since the Man in the Suit was sincere in his mission, and since the Company and the government already knew about the existence of the Bigfoots, I decided it couldn't hurt to show him the Bigfoot village so he could see firsthand the people being harmed by the destruction of the local rainforest.

I was shocked when we arrived. What had been before a shambles was now a neat little settlement. Sarai, having taken advantage of her celebrity status, had put the Bigfoots to work fixing up their shelters and sweeping out all the debris. She even appeared to have gotten them to take a bath!

The Bigfoots were surprisingly unconcerned about the Man in the Suit.

I guess they had seen enough in the past week to make them a little jaded. Possibly their interactions with Sarai had made them see that not all Humans were bad, scrawny and hairless though they may be.

"You know," said the Man in the Suit, "maybe the problem isn't development so much as..."

He looked around as if searching for something, quickly spying a Bigfoot with his thumb in a gourd,

"They're trying to use fleas as money." He finished with a flourish, as if making an fundamental point.

I didn't see where this was a problem, until he related an incident of some weeks prior when a lone Bigfoot with a gourdful of fleas had entered a remote general store trying to buy some roasted meat.

Things evidently didn't go as the Bigfoot had expected, and it ended up trashing the store and running off with the entire spit of meat, still in the cooker.

"There is some interest in the fleas as fishing bait" said the Man in the Suit, eyeing a group of Bigfoot's busily throwing bones, "But I have to tell you, it's somewhat limited."

He set down his briefcase and popped it open.

"Perhaps there's a way we can help the Bigfoots obtain some of the things they are clearly wanting," said the Man in the Suit, "And still manage the land so that they can live in peace."

The Man in the Suit began to produce various trinkets and goodies from his surprisingly roomy briefcase, handing them out, along with extra-large business cards, as he introduced himself to several of the Bigfoots.

The Bigfoot males immediately started fighting over the notebook-sized strips of dried, seasoned meat known as "teriyaki flavored beef jerky", while the Bigfoot Wives were extremely interested in the strings of large plastic beads. (I wasn't sure why they even wanted the gaudy beads, dull as they were compared to their miraculous eyelashes, but they immediately placed them around their necks and promenaded proudly through the village.)

For the Bigfoot children he produced a soccer ball which he inflated using a bicycle pump.

I was starting wonder if bringing the Man in the Suit to the village was really such a good idea after all, but Sarai took the broader view:

"Sure, it's disruptive," Sarai said. "In an ideal world, Humans and Bigfoots would never intersect. But the world's getting smaller every day, and soon there won't be any places left to retreat to. At least now the government knows they're here and can take measures to protect them."

It was hard to tell if Sarai really meant what she was saying or if she was merely trying to cheer me up. It was, after all, consistent with her worldview—the focus of her work being to discover and catalogue new species in order to save them.

As for the cheering up part, she could clearly see that wasn't working.

"It was probably going to happen at some point anyway," she continued. "Imagine how things might have turned out if we *hadn't* stumbled into the middle of it. At least now we have hope that, given all the facts, people will do the right thing."

Being a student of Human history, I was not so optimistic, but instead I merely said, "And failing that, there's always the forest monster."

Sarai gave me a quizzical look.

"I'll explain later." I sighed.

"Darn right you will!" She exclaimed, jumping on me and digging her fingers deep into my fur. "But right now, I think someone needs a hug!"

I couldn't see how that would help anything, but she squeezed me with all of her might, and you know what? It did make things a little bit better.

EPILOGUE

We crossed the equator just as the full moon, golden and resplendent, reached its zenith at the stroke of midnight. We'd timed it that way, planning weeks in advance, and it was well worth the wait.

The jungle around us was quiet—quiet, at least, as jungles get, which isn't really that quiet at all, but a tapestry of sound—the insects singing in their oversized voices, nocturnal creatures calling as they foraged in the darkness, the ever-gentle rustle of the breezes in the treetops, and the creaking of their branches as they swayed upon the air— wrapping around us like a favorite old blanket.

Since I am a Yeti, seven feet tall and possessing certain powers, no predator in the forest is interested in me. Or if they are, they quickly come to think better of it, even the mighty boa constrictor which fears no man or beast. This is very good for my companion, Sarai, who is a good deal shorter and decidedly human. Not that Sarai is afraid of anything—if she were she never would have chosen her profession which entails traveling the remotest wilds to catalogue new species—just that for a jaguar or a boa constrictor, she would make a tempting meal. At the moment however, Sarai was sitting snug against me, gazing in awe at the full moon's effulgence.

"Crazy, you can see the moon a million times and never lose your sense of wonder." murmured Sarai.

How long we sat it was easy to tell, for I tracked the moon as it made its descent toward the western horizon, and though it seemed a mere moment, it was a moment lasting a fraction of forever, which is an infinity, and incalculably precious—for all the moments remaining in our lives, we would never regain this particular one, except in our memory.

Sarai rustled softly against me in her sleep.

The jungle was so bright—the moonlight sparkling in the barest glints of moisture in the uncharacteristically desiccate air. Being dryer than usual, the jungle had taken on a brittle veneer, and you could see a lot farther than you'd normally be able to—the night had taken on an almost crystalline clarity.

My pupils must have been as big as pies, having most of the night to adjust.

Though I have never seen a pie, Sarai has mentioned them often, being evidently very fond of them. They sound excellent from the way she describes them, and I mean to try one as soon as we get to the United States, where I am told they are something of a cultural icon.

She speaks of these pies especially on those long, lean nights in the forest when foraging is not as bounteous as one would wish, naming all the endless varieties. I very much hope especially to try a chocolate pie when we reach Louisiana.

On this night however, the foraging was plentiful, and both Sarai and I had gorged ourselves on luscious, ripe fruits and delicious, fresh nuts.

I was just starting to drift off to sleep when I heard a sort of scratchy-squeaky cough from off in the jungle, followed by a long, satisfied sigh.

For a just second I thought I caught the gleam of two small, red eyes.

I nudged the sleeping Sarai.

"I think we've attracted a follower."

"That's nice." Said Sarai, snuggling into a more comfortable position. "I'll have to bake him a pie."

She was already back asleep, happily dreaming, so I settled back, let out a contented sigh, and finally closed my eyes.

Just for an hour, I promised myself.

Just until sunrise.

Acknowledgements

I would like to thank Connor and Brooke for being my first readers, editor Eric for his unwavering support, and my many myriad friends, especially the crew at the Flat Black Coffee shop in Lower Mills, Dorchester, MA, who provided not only with an uninterrupted supply of fair-trade, hand-roasted coffee, but willing ears upon which to ply my story until I finally got it straight.

Additionally I would like to thank Daniel Manus Pinkwater (by many considered among the finest authors of the age) whose books (which include "The Last Guru", "Lizard Music" and "Alan Mendelsohn, the Boy from Mars") are sheer delight.

Finally I would like to thank Clea, my best friend, who taught me that sometimes kissing a dog is the highest expression of loving friendship.

∞

Or are they?

Sakteng Wildlife Sanctuary, Bhutan

Google it!

original photo as seen on Google Earth
27° 18' 58.00" N   91° 54' 32.89" E
Photographer: Padam B Chuwan

ABOUT THE AUTHOR

MJ's relationship with mythology began at the age of five with
the discovery of D'Aulaire's classic "Book of Norse Myths"
and has never waned. After a decade in high tech,
MJ retired to research and write full-time.
MJ has a degree in Classical Studies
from Boston University,
and enjoys hiking
and fresh
air.

☯

☯ the Yeti Chronicles ☯

www.ingramcontent.com/pod-product-compliance
Lightning Source LLC
Chambersburg PA
CBHW021102130626
46554CB00002B/495